Praise for the Detective Tommy Keane series:

"Detective Tommy Keane is one true-blue streetwise cop. But what makes him exceptional is his honest soul. That's a combination that can keep you turning the pages deep into the night."

- Jay Schadler, 20/20, ABC News, Nightline, Good Morning America, and National Geographic.

"From the streets of the Bronx to the Upper East Side, Sister Margaret, offers a tantalizing glimpse of NYC crime where nothing is ever what it seems, and fighting it is anything but routine."
- NYPD Police Commissioner, Dermot Shea.

"Devious intense and disturbing."   -
Zoe Williams, whatsbetterthanbooks.com   Best Book Blog 2017.

"You can't get any more New York than Detective Tommy Keane. Reading this series is like walking in the shoes, and seeing through the eyes of a man who embodies the city, nail-biting, shocking, and fascinating, these stories are the real deal - and highly addictive."

-Meg MacCary, Desperately Seeking the 80's Podcast.

"A gut punch of a tale that takes the reader behind the crime scene tape and onto an exhilarating tour of the streets, drug dens, dive bars and precinct houses of New York City, with an insiders view that rarely makes the papers."
- Jesse Smith, Crime Journalist, Kingston Times.

"The Myers Siblings create real, raw, heart wrenching crime fiction like no one else in this genre."
– Kayla Waters, True Crime Exposed Podcast.

Tommy Keane is the man! Travis and Natasha write their books in a way that makes it easy to follow yet gives you great detail and keeps you wanting more! They are absolutely my favorite crime authors of all time!
- Sam Sprunger, The 500 Section Lounge Podcast.

"NYPD Detective Travis Myers spent years "on the job" in the Bronx. Now, Travis and his sister Natasha, bring to life the escapades of fictional detective Tommy Keane in these fast-paced police procedurals."
- Peabody Award-Winning Investigative Reporter, Host of the True Crime Reporter Podcast, Robert Riggs.

"Authentic and engaging crime fiction."
– Sandra Mangan, crimefictionlover.com

"An exciting and interesting read, loaded with plot twists, consider me an official Tommy Keane fan!"
– Suzie Que, Punkoleum Magazine.

SOL ABRAMOWITZ

**Also by Travis Myers
&
Natasha Myers Marsiguerra**

Sister Margaret

Hayden Jon Marshall

Jenny Black

Li Jun

A Fairly Violent Life

SOL ABRAMOWITZ

A Tommy Keane Novel

Travis Myers &
Natasha Myers Marsiguerra

Published in the United States by Bully Press Corp.

Bully Press Corp
P. O. Box 404
Wingdale, NY 12594 United States
www.bullypress.net

Cover design by: Phred Rawles

ISBN-13: 979-8-9890119-2-6

For the clean-up team:

Mary, Rosemarie, Christine, Henry, Maryrose,

And Kristina.

***

Dedicated to every Cop and Detective, in every city, in every country on the planet. Thank you for standing on the side of right, and for fighting the good and never-ending fight against those who would destroy all we hold dear.

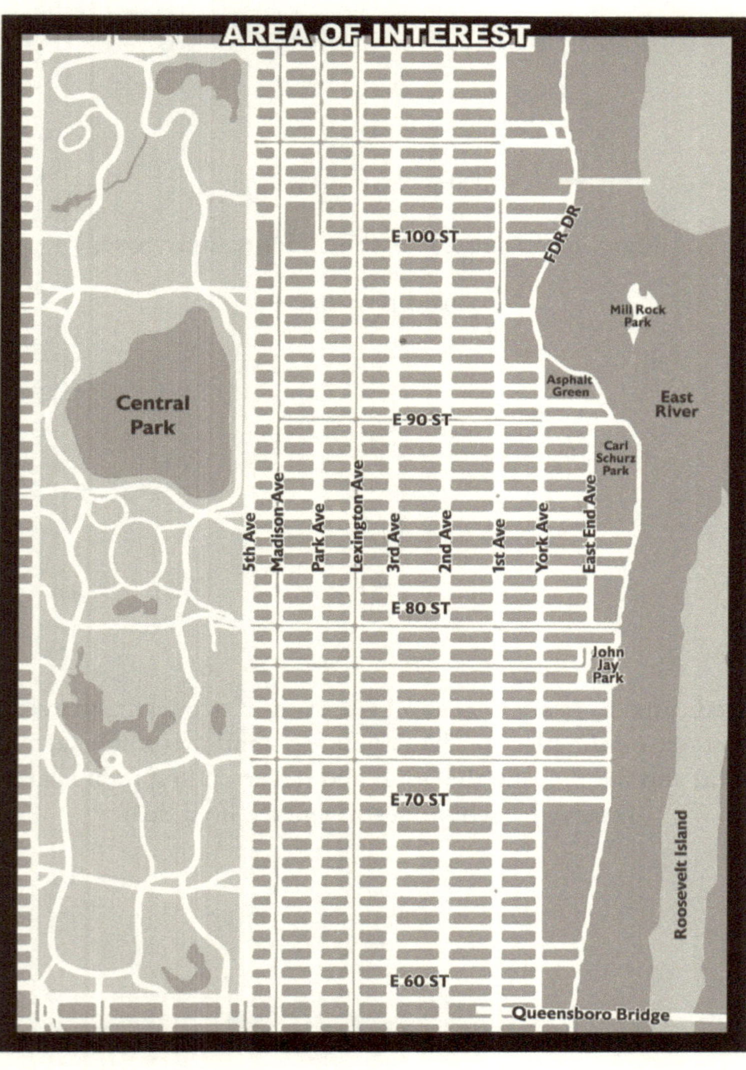

AREA OF INTEREST
Central Park
E 100 ST
E 90 ST
E 80 ST
E 70 ST
E 60 ST
5th Ave
Madison Ave
Park Ave
Lexington Ave
3rd Ave
2nd Ave
1st Ave
York Ave
East End Ave
FDR DR
Mill Rock Park
Asphalt Green
East River
Carl Schurz Park
John Jay Park
Roosevelt Island
Queensboro Bridge

"It is sometimes an appropriate response to reality to go insane."

~Phillip K. Dick – Author.

Prologue

Officers Tommy Keane and Henry Sanchez were on patrol, working sector-Charlie in the 5-3 precinct, on a cool October afternoon. They had just finished their meal at the New Capital Diner on Kingsbridge Road.

As Tommy turned their patrol car north onto Jerome Avenue, Henry slapped him on the arm.

"Hey, Tommy, get a load of this." Pointing out the window.

Three young teenage males were taunting a topless woman, who was spinning a mop handle around her head like a cowboy would twirl a lasso, attempting to hit anyone that got too close, all the while screaming obscenities at the three.

WOOP! WOOP! Went the siren as Henry hit the button twice and Tommy pulled up the car to the curb. The three miscreants quickly took off south and turned the corner onto Kingsbridge Road, leaving the crazed woman still screaming and swinging her stick at anyone who came near her.

Henry put a radio call into central as they climbed out of the car.

"5-3 Charlie central, we got a 10-10, possible crime or EDP (Emotionally Disturbed Person) northeast corner of Jerome and Kingsbridge, Topless female, White, possibly Hispanic, 25-45 years of age, screaming and swinging a stick, will advise…"

"10-4 copy 5-3 Charlie, 10-10 EDP Jerome and Kingsbridge."

Tommy slowly approached the woman, both hands up showing her his palms,

"You okay, miss? Can I help you in any way?"

The woman made eye contact and it was obvious she was completely out of her mind. She kept screaming while spit bubbled and dripped out of her mouth.

"Stay back, cop! I'll take your eye out with this if you come any closer!" She shrieked back at him like a woman possessed.

A voice came over the radio, "5-3 Adam Central, be advised, tell sector Charlie if the women's name is Annie, she is a fighter and a biter! Sector Adam en route to assist."

"10-4, Adam, 5-3 Charlie, be advised, EDP may be violent, possible biter, known as Annie. 5-3 Adam en-route."

"10-4, copy that central."

Tommy who had never encountered this woman before, immediately asked, "What's your name, dear?"

The woman growled back unintelligibly.

"Come on, honey, I'm here to help you not hurt you, I just wanna keep you safe," Tommy said in a soft kind voice.

"I'm… Annie!" she said loudly, but not quite as manic as before, raising her stick up over her head slightly more than it was while taking on a more threatening stance.

Tommy quickly determined how he would attempt to de-escalate the situation and calm this woman out of her mania, "Annie, Annie don't you remember me, honey?" Tommy asked, again, softly and gently like before.

Annie cocked her head and squinted her eye's a little bit trying to recognize this man who she had never seen before.

"No!" she shouted, and Tommy stepped a couple steps closer. As he did, Henry began to move to his right in order to get behind Annie, but Tommy motioned with his hand to wait.

"Really, Annie? C-mon, are you telling me you really can't remember me? We were friends when we were little kids, it's me, Tommy. C-mon, Annie you have to remember me."

Annie's shoulders loosened up and dropped from their defensive, pre-attack posture, and she looked deep into Tommy's eyes, "Tommy?"

"Yes." Tommy replied as he stepped closer, and Annie lowered her stick to her waist still holding it tightly with both hands.

"C-mon, Annie, put the stick down, you know I would never hurt you in a million years, and besides we gotta get you covered up, look at you, your jumblies are hanging out all over the place, and you have no shoes on… aren't you cold, honey?"

Henry laughed a bit to himself when Tommy said "Jumblies," referring to her naked breasts, and again Tommy motioned with his hand for Henry to stay back and be cool.

Annie's body language softened, still locked in a steady gaze into Tommy's dark brown eyes, the metal end of the mop handle clanked and bounced as it hit the concrete of the sidewalk.

"There you go, that's my girl, Annie…"

As Tommy stepped closer Henry spoke into his radio, "5-3 Charlie central, EDP under control, please send a bus (Ambulance) Northeast corner of Jerome and Kingsbridge."

"10-4 5-3 Charlie."

As Henry lowered his radio, 5-3 Adam pulled up and Officers Michael Norton and Eddie Briggs exited their vehicles and walked up next to where Henry was standing.

"I see you boys broke your cherries with our Crazy Annie, and woo, look at her today, all sexy and looking to meet!" Eddie Briggs said to Henry. The three officers were about twenty feet from where Tommy and Annie stood.

"We are friends, aren't we?" Annie asked.

"Of course we are, Annie, do you remember me now?"

"Yes, yes, you're, your name is…"

"Tommy, Tommy from your old block, you do remember me, Annie, oh, I'm so happy to see you again, dear, it's been so long, and I was a little sad to think you didn't remember me." Tommy was only placating her insanity, but it was comforting to her, and Annie began to respond with acceptance rather than fear and violence.

"I remember you, Tommy – Tommy, Tommy, Tommy, I remember you now, of course I do!" Annie said with a big smile, drool still rolling out of her mouth.

"Annie… My dear friend, listen, it is way too cold, and you are way to naked to be out here like this, would you like to have a seat in my car?"

Annie furrowed her brow, looking at the patrol car, then back at Tommy with a hint of anger and distrust.

"No! No police, no police cars!"

"Annie." Tommy began, firmer than before but still in a gentle voice and demeanor, "I just want to get you into a nice warm place, and out of the cold, I'm not trying to pull a fast one… You believe me, don't you? You know I would never hurt you, you're my dear friend Annie, c-mon, get in my car where it's nice and warm."

"I know, I know, Tommy, you're my friend, right? I know you don't want to hurt me…O-Okay, we can go."

Tommy put his arm out, with his elbow bent, "Come on, honey, let's get in the car and warm you up."

Annie took his arm, and they began to walk towards the patrol car. Henry, along with officers, Norton and Briggs, stepped back away from the vehicle to give Annie and Tommy plenty of room. Annie stood up straight and stuck her bare chest out with pride, as she and Tommy made their way to the vehicle and he opened the door for her, like the lady she was.

***

Annie Assante was a resident schizophrenic, who lived her entire thirty-two years in the neighborhood and spent nearly all her days in a daycare program some ten blocks north of where she now sat in the rear of a patrol car. Her nights and weekends were spent at home in the care of her mother and father. Annie was known to escape from the daycare on a semi-regular basis, as well as to have violent outbursts when not on her medication.

Although only thirty-two, Annies poor physical condition and unkempt hair and clothing, made her look as though she could easily be in her mid-fifties. She was well-known as a regular call for the men and women of the 5-3, who would often have to physically restrain her before taking her into custody and subsequently transporting her by patrol car, or by ambulance, to NCB (North Central Bronx) Hospital.

***

"Look at you, you charming bastard," Eddie Briggs said after Tommy closed the car door with Annie now seated inside, "Someone's got a way with the ladies, last couple times we had to bring Crazy Annie in, it was a fight into the car, and then a fight into the hospital, good for you, Keane, you tamed a savage beast here."

And before the conversation could continue the ambulance pulled up and Tommy asked Annie to get back out of the car.

"No, Tommy, no, I want to stay with you!" Annie said, and Eddie Briggs laughed.

"Fuck you, Briggsy!" Annie shouted, then spit at him in contempt.

"Annie!" Tommy said firmly, "That's not my girl, c-mon now be nice!"

"Sorry, but I hate him!"

"C-mon, let's go, Annie, the ambulance is here for you."

"No! I want to stay with you, you're nice, Tommy!"

"You can't, Annie, I must go back to work, and you can't come… I'll tell you what though? If you come along nice and behave, I'll take a ride in the ambulance with you to the hospital," Annie's face lit up, "But you have to be good when we get there, and you absolutely have to be good to the nurses when they take you in, okay?"

"Okay! Okay, if you ride with me, you said you'll ride with me?"

"Oh yeah! I'm gonna ride with you, but then you have to be good for the nurses, okay, promise?"

"Promise!" and Annie and Tommy linked their pinkies making it a sacred oath.

"And know, Annie, they're all my friends over there at the hospital, so don't misbehave or they'll tell me you were bad."

"I won't, Tommy, I promise."

And with that, they again hooked arms and Tommy led her to the rear of the ambulance, where a heavy-set female EMT helped Annie step up into the ambulance and wrapped her topless body in a blanket. She strapped her into the gurney and took her vitals as Tommy rode with them the half mile or so to NCB Hospital.

Both Tommy and Henry would have a few more meetings with Annie over the years, as would most every other officer working the 5-3 at some time, and many of them picked up the habit of telling Annie, "Behave Annie or I'll tell Tommy on you." And nine times out of ten, it would actually work.

As time went on, Annie began to respond less aggressively whenever confronted by the police, even to Eddie Briggs, who she said she hated. Annie would also relentlessly ask officers if they knew Tommy, or if they had seen him lately, as it turned out his kindness and understanding left an indelible mark on her psyche and did indeed tame some of Annies violent outbursts.

Chapter One

It was Tommy's first day back to work at the 21st Precinct. Just four weeks prior he had been shot in front of his apartment building in White Plains, by members of the Purple Dragon gang, during the Li Jun investigation. His injuries were all healed, he had gotten plenty of rest, had been hitting the gym regularly, and was feeling quite fit and eager to return to the 2-1 to get back to work.

As he approached the entrance to the precinct he stopped and looked up at the façade of the building, took a deep breath and smiled to himself. Yes, he was happy to return to work and looked forward to what the day would have in store for him.

As he entered the building, Sergeant Ruffalo, looked up from the desk and gave Tommy a warm smile, "Welcome back, Detective."

"Thanks, Sarge." Tommy replied.

As he made it to the second-floor hallway, Charice Tate, the squad PAA, (Police Administrative Assistant.) stood up from her desk that was stationed just outside the squad room and squealed with excitement at the site of Tommy, as he stepped onto the landing.

"Oh, Tommy, my sweet Tommy Keane, Charice is so happy to see your handsome ass making it back in here where it belongs! And look at you, just look at you, handsome and healthy as ever!" She continued, as she stepped from behind her desk and gave him a huge hug, "God bless you, Detective, I am so so happy you are alright, and so so happy to see you back here again where you belong!"

"Thank you, Charice, it's good to be back, and so nice to see your beautiful smile again too."

Charice placed her hands on Tommy's cheeks and looked deep into his eyes, "Now you be careful from now on you hear me? You are too dear to me for me to be losing you, you hear me?" Then she gave him another big hug and pushed him toward the door to the squad room giving him a slap on the ass as she did.

Tommy stepped into the squad room and upon entering saw Detective Mark Stein, the same as he ever was, sitting at his desk, his face covered by the newspaper he was reading. Detective Jimmy Coletti, with his back toward him, was fixing himself a cup of coffee, and Detective Doreen Doyle, sitting at her desk looking through a book of mug shots… After a few seconds, Doreen looked up from her book and saw Tommy standing in the doorway in a long tan wool overcoat looking back at her. She lowly addressed Mark,

"Well look what the cat dragged in Mark; do you remember this guy?"

Mark lowered his paper and looked over the top of his glasses that sat low on his nose at Tommy, "Yeah he looks familiar." He said sarcastically while also winking at Tommy, then raising his paper back up covering his face once again.

"Hey guys, how yous doing?" Tommy asked.

Colletti turned and with a big, excited smile, stuttered out "T-T-T-Tommy!"

Then Doreen began, "What's that, Detective? How are we doing? You know you wouldn't have to ask that if you had checked in at all over the past four weeks, or maybe answered a message or two there, Mr. Man… We, for the most part, are doing very well, the question is how have you been there tough guy, mister too cool to call and let us know what we can do for you, or let us know how you're feeling?"

"I'm sorry, Doreen, it's been, well, I'm fine, I just took the time off you know, really just went to my appointments and the gym, and kind of kept to myself, it was good, I feel great, I'm sorry for not being in touch."

Doreen stood from her seat and walked over to Tommy, "Fuck you, Keane," she said as she put her hand up to Tommy's head and ran her thumb over the scar that lie beneath his hair where he had been shot just weeks before, then tightly wrapped her arms around him, whispering "I fucking missed you." Before releasing her embrace.

"I'm sorry, Doreen, I know I should have checked in, and it was selfish of me not to."

As they chatted, Lieutenant Bricks stepped from his office, "Tommy!... Good to see you back, how you feeling, pal?"

"Never been better, Lu, feeling really good."

"Excellent, well it's good to have you back, Tom, let me know if there's anything you need, also… You three… keep your mouths shut," he directed that part toward Mark, Jimmy, and Doreen, then looking back in Tommy's direction, "There should be a nice surprise arriving soon for you, Tom."

"Surprise?"

"Yeah, well don't get excited, it's not a gift or anything, just a little something I think/hope, you're gonna like?"

"Hmmm? Okay, well, I'm looking forward to it… I think?"

Tommy picked up a stack of his still open cases and sat at Detective Keogh's desk and began thumbing through them, "Fuck me, I have some catching up to do." He said aloud as he began addressing each case one by one.

About ten minutes, or so, had past, when a deep, loud, voice from behind Tommy's back shook the small squad room.

"Two Gun Tommy Keane!" Tommy recognized the voice, but it took a moment to register, "There he is, my man! They told me you'd be draggin' your sorry ass back in here this week, and here you are!"

Tommy spun around in his chair and leapt to his feet when he saw it was his old, and very dear friend, Clarence (Clay) Johnson. Tommy and Clay were in the Police Academy together, both had started their careers in the 5-3, served on the same Anti-Crime team together, and joined the Bronx Narcotics Division during the same period but were assigned to different teams. They knew each other before either were married, or either had children, their relationship was one of love and respect and loaded with history.

"Clay! Holy shit!" the two men embraced each other with a hardy slap onto one another backs, "Good to see you man! Wow, so this is the surprise?" Tommy asked the room in general.

Lieutenant Bricks stuck his head out of his office and smiled, happy to witness the reunion.

"So, what you doing here brother?" Tommy asked, "Are you…"

"Yes, sir! I am newly assigned to the 2-1 Detective Squad!"

"Ahh man, that's great!"

"Fuck yeah! Da Bronx is in da house! Keane and Johnson, together again!" Clay said loudly with a big smile on his face.

Again, they hugged and traded the same slap slap on one another's backs.

Mark, Doreen, Jimmy, and Lieutenant Bricks all smiled as they watched these two men gush over one another like two schoolgirls reunited after a long summer break, then Doreen chimed in,

"Two Gun Tommy Keane? Is that what you guys called him up in the Bronx? Sounds like there's a story there?"

"No no no, there's no story there, and nobody called me that but this clown." Tommy protested.

"Hells yeah, there's a story there," Clay replied in a very emphatic manner.

"Really?" Doreen became excited "Story time! sto-ry time, sto-ry time!" She began to chant.

"No no, there's no story here, stop now." Tommy again said in protest.

"C-mon now, if there's a story, I'm sure we'd all like to hear it?" Said Lieutenant Bricks.

"Looks like you're outranked there, Tommy," said Mark, "Go ahead, Clay, tell us why our friend and colleague carries this moniker of Two Gun Tommy Keane?"

Clay began. He was a tall, broad man with a booming voice, and he slowly raised his large hands and motioned with both of them, as if to beckon everyone to come closer, then lowering his voice a bit as if he were addressing a class of young grade school children, he told this story.

"Now, you all know Tommy and I worked in the Bronx together, and at the time of this particular story, we was both on the 5-3 Anti-Crime Team. And on this night, we was working with Tommy's regular partner, the fearless Henry Sanchez, and I was driving our boss, Sergeant Ray Amador. We were doing a 6 to 2 shift, and we started out our night at the New Capitol Diner on Jerome Avenue, you know the whole eat while you can thing, then we headed out to find us some bad guys."

"We did a few car stops, and a few stop and frisks but nothing worthwhile. Then a call came over the radio about a home invasion that took place over on Grand Avenue, where the inhabitants were robbed, and a possible rape occurred. Central gave a description of three armed Dominican men, mid-twenties in a blue BMW, no plates noted. Well, we kept doing what we were doing, but we all had that description in our heads, right. Well, now it's later, a couple-few hours go by right, streets are quieting down, and Henry comes over the radio to us point to point, so we can only talk to each other with no outside interference and says that him and Tommy are behind a blue BMW with what looked like three men inside heading north on Jerome Avenue."

"Ray and I were like two blocks away and headed over to Jerome and got behind them, and now all three cars are headed north. We decided Tommy and Henry would pull ahead and cut the BMW off and we'd get behind it basically trapping it between us right."

"So, as we're approaching Bedford Park Boulevard, the BMW pulls into the right lane, Tommy guns it and cuts in front of the BMW. I pull up close behind it, we got em, they're stuck between our two cars, and on the left by one of the big ass iron beams that hold up the El Train, they're trapped, got nowhere to go right?"

"So, we all hop out of our cars guns drawn, screamin' at these motherfuckers, you know, Police don't move! Let me see your hands! All that shit right. Well, these motherfuckers are some bad ass motherfuckers and all three come out blazing, I mean bang, bang bang bang bang, all three of em are just letting loose at all four of us, bullets flyin' everywhere, glass breaking, rounds tearing through our cars. Then as I let one round go, I get hit in my left leg and knocked to the ground."

"Ray and Henry are returning fire and they both hit the motherfucker who exited the passenger side of the vehicle. As the other two bolted from the driver's side across Jerome Avenue towards the entrance of the 4 train. So, my sorry ass is layin in the middle of Jerome Avenue in a pool of my own blood, cause yeah, I got a big ass hole in my leg, and as I'm layin there I let another round go, and catch one of them two in the ankle and he goes down, but not without a fight, because he's down but still shooting. Then this fucker here," He looks and points at Tommy, "Like he's in some old school John Wayne western movie, walks… Yeah, motherfucker walks, as cool as cool could be across Jerome Avenue, he's got his little .38 revolver in his left hand and his .9mm pistol in his right, and -Bang! He shoots the guy who's laying in the street one time with the .38, hitting him in the throat and ending his ass, then Bang! Bang! He lets two rounds go from his nine and he drops the other motherfucker who was firing back from maybe 30 yards away, over near the stairs of the 4 train."

"Then, almost in slow motion I watch this man here turn, he's got no emotion on his face, there's gun smoke particles being caught in the street lights around him, and that acrid, metallic, sulphury smell in the air, ya'll know that smell, and yeah, like in slow motion he walks over to me still with a gun in each hand and asks, in a calm cool voice, You alright Clay? then turns and asks Ray, if he's called a bus for me yet."

"Whoa! And what did you say?" Jimmy asked like a wide-eyed kid at a Marvel attraction at Disney.

"Well, I wasn't nearly so cool as Two Gun, here, and I kinda screamed something like, 'Nah, I ain't alright, I got a hole in my leg motherfucker!' And that ladies and gentlemen is why we calls him -Two Gun Tommy Keane… The coolest gun in the west!"

"Now that was a great story! And I loved how you told it too!" Jimmy said excitedly.

"Hell yeah, tell us another one, Clay, we wanna hear more about Two-Gun!" Doreen chimed in.

"Okay, first off nobody in the world calls me that except for this jerk face, and story time is over." Tommy interjected.

"I remember when that happened." Said Lieutenant Bricks.

"So do I," Mark added, "I was working special victims at the time, and I remember how we couldn't believe how it only got like two minutes on the news, and I think only the Herald covered in the paper, and even then, it was just a blurb like six to eight pages in."

"That's cause it was in the boogie down, you know nothing that happens in the Bronx makes the papers or the TV, but hell, had them three armed robber rapists done that shit here in Manhattan, that shit would have been national news." Said Clay.

Jimmy shook his head, "Wow, incredible story, thanks for telling it to us, maybe you give us more when Tommy ain't here to stop you?"

Clay winked at Jimmy and things calmed a bit after story time, and all five detectives got back to work.

***

8:12 PM

Lieutenant Bricks stuck his head out of the office to find only Tommy, Doreen, and Clay, present.

"Who's catching tonight?"

"I am, Lu." Clay answered.

"Alright, we got a body, sounds like an elderly man was assaulted and killed on 6-6 and York, you three head over there asap, and I'll get ahold of Jimmy and Mark, and have them meet you over there."

Chapter Two

8:26 PM

The three detectives arrived on scene at the south side of East 66th Street about twenty feet west of York Avenue. Patrol had already taped off the corner with police tape, and they were met by Sergeant Diaz, as they approached.

"Detective Keane, good to see you back pal, how you feelin'?

"Feelin' good, Sarge, how you been?"

"Been good, been real good, just found out we're having another kid, and I couldn't be happier."

"Really? Good for you man, happy to hear that."

"This body yours Keane?"

"No sir, my good friend here Clay, will be taking this one."

Sergeant Diaz stuck his hand out and nodded his head, "Detective."

"How you doin'. Sergeant Diaz? Clay, Clay Johnson." Clay replied as both men shook hands.

"Good to meet you, Clay – and how are you doing Doreen?" Sergeant Diaz asked, turning himself to the side to get a look at Doreen around Clay's broad frame.

"Good, Sarge, better than that poor fella on the sidewalk over there, that's for sure."

"What do we know so far, Sergeant?" Clay asked.

"Elderly male, Jewish, looks and sounds like he took a couple whacks with some sort of blunt weapon. We have two witnesses for you, I'm happy to say, both have the same description, but are real weak on any details. They both say it just happened too fast."

"How you know he's Jewish?" Clay asked.

"He's wearing a yarmulke, so I took a guess…" Sgt Diaz motioned his head in the direction of the body, "Come take a look."

The three detectives slipped under the police tape and stood around the body. They took a moment, and all stared at the victim, a tall white-haired older gentleman, in a black nylon overcoat, and a dark navy suit. A navy yarmulke was pinned atop his head with hairpins, a broken pair of horned-rimmed glasses still on his face, his brown eyes open behind them. Two gashes were on his forehead, and neither appeared to be caused by his fall onto the sidewalk.

Clay and Tommy then donned some latex gloves and began a search of the body, with Clay immediately reaching into the dead gentleman's rear pocket and retrieving his wallet.

"Solomon Abramowitz, looks like he's… Seventy-nine years old, lives a couple of blocks over on 71st Street."

Tommy pulled a small bundle of bills from Mr. Abramowitz's front right pants pocket, "56 Dollars."

Tommy ran his hand around the back of the victim's head and found another gash, raising his bloody gloved hand to show Clay and Doreen.

"Whatever he was hit with opened up the back of his head pretty good, too."

Then the three of them paused for a moment, and again all stared down at Mr. Abramowitz, then all simultaneously looked around at the surroundings.

"Doesn't look like a robbery, what you guys think?" Clay asked.

"Maybe a robbery gone wrong?" Doreen answered.

"Let's interview our witnesses, see what they can add," said Tommy, continuing to run his eyes over the victim as he spoke.

Sergeant Diaz walked Clay and Tommy over to the entrance of a building where the two witnesses, Ina Gardner, a seventy-year-old woman who stood only five feet tall and wore a long dark blue woolen coat with a black velvet collar, and a much taller Maureen O'Meara, sixty-two, who wore a black bubble jacket over teal scrubs, that were tucked into black Uggs, stood inside the door of the vestibule with a uniformed officer to keep warm as they waited.

As the men entered the building Sergeant Diaz began; "Hello ladies, as I mentioned earlier here are the detectives who would like to ask each of you what exactly it was you witnessed earlier, this is Detective Clay Johnson, and Detective Thomas Keane, Gentlemen, I'll leave you to it."

"Thomas Keane? I have heard of you, you're the young man who saved that boy on Thanksgiving aren't you?" Ina Gardener asked.

"Yes ma'am, that was my case."

"Oh, how exciting!" She replied, as if she had met an actual celebrity.

Tommy smiled at her, and she smiled back, "Please Ms. Gardener, tell my friend Clay, Detective Johnson, what you saw happen to our victim, Ms. O'Meara step outside with me for a moment if you will, so these two can speak in private, please."

"Yes, sir" she replied, and they both stepped out onto the sidewalk so Clay could interview Ina Gardner.

"So, Mrs. Gardner, I'm sorry is it Mrs. Gardner?"

"Yes, Detective, for forty-six years now I've been Mrs. Gardner,"

"Very nice, my wife and I just made eighteen years ourselves. Can you please Mrs. Gardner, and take your time dear, tell me exactly what you saw this evening, take your time, and try to remember everything, no matter how small it may seem."

"Eighteen years, how nice, and good for you, so many young people get divorced these days, and so many never even get married to begin with, so sad, but good for you, Detective… Well, now where to start, well, I was walking home. I, I had been to visit my friend, my dear friend Shiela, who lives just around the corner, poor dear, she's been quite lonely since she lost her husband last year, so, so I was walking home, and I watched a man, a tall man, he had on a black leather jacket, and dark hair, run up behind the older gentleman and hit him with something from behind. The older man let out one loud yell and fell to the floor, and the tall man in the jacket hit him two or three more times with whatever he had, a stick or a pipe or a bat I don't know? Then he ran off, it was quite frightening, and happened so very fast."

"Okay, did the tall man in the leather jacket say anything? Did you hear him say anything to the older gentleman?"

"He said, F you, several times, well at least two or three times? I'm sorry I'm not exactly sure, but that is the only thing I heard him say."

"Oh no, nothing to be sorry about, you're doing great, can you give me more of a description? More about what this tall man looked like, the clothes he was wearing, his ethnicity, was he black, white or brown skinned, since you heard him yell, was there any sort of discernable accent you could recognize?"

"Yes, he had, a black leather jacket, it was short, stopped at his waist, he was white, I'm pretty sure he was white, he had dark hair, combed straight back, almost like a pompadour, it's possible he could be Puerto Rican, but I think he was white, and I think dark jeans or pants, I'm sorry I don't know? And his voice, gee, all he said was F you, and I will say, all I can say it was loud and very angry but confident, if that helps you at all, Detective Johnson?"

"Yes, ma'am it does, it gets me started dear, how tall would you say?"

"About six feet tall, and thin, he was thin."

"Perfect, thank you, here is my card, if you think of anything at all please call me, we have your information, and I may call you in the future to follow up, but otherwise you are free to go Mrs. Gardner, thank you so much for your time."

"Thank you, Detective." She replied with a kind smile as she nodded her head and then went on her way.

Clay opened the door for her to leave the entry way and simultaneously asked Mrs. O'Meara to join him, he then began with the same question,

"What can you tell me about what you saw this evening?"

"I was coming from work, I'm a nurse at New York Hospital, and as I stepped up onto the curb, I hear a loud 'Fuck you! Fuck you! Which startled me and I looked up to see a man, looked like a white guy, it happened so fast I really didn't see much but I saw this guy knock the old man to the sidewalk then hit him two to four times in the head with what looked like a white stick then take off, whole thing was like literally 3-4 seconds, so yeah, a white guy, maybe 30 years old? About six foot? 175 pounds? Black motorcycle jacket, dark blue maybe black jeans, dark hair I think, it was really quick, and the guy ran away like a shot."

"Okay, black motorcycle jacket, can you describe it?"

"Yeah, you know, a typical black leather motorcycle jacket, you know with the zipper pockets, zippers on the sleeves and the belt."

"Right, I know exactly what you're talking about now."

"Yeah, you know like Sha Na Na, would have worn back in the day."

"Ha, Sha Na Na, the 50's cover band, I remember that show from TV, my father used to watch it, now there's a blast from the past… Here take my card, if you think of anything else you can share with me please give me a call, anytime, we have your info, and if I need to I may be contacting you soon as well, but otherwise you have a good night Mrs. O'Meara."

"Yes, sir, Detective, you too, and please catch this piece of shit soon, I hate to think of this animal striking again,"

"Yes, ma'am we definitely plan to!"

***

Clay and Tommy walked back to where Mr. Abramowitz' body lay and Doreen and Sergeant Diaz stood chatting over it, they could see Detectives Mark Stien and Jimmy Coletti exit their vehicle and make their way over to the body themselves.

The five detectives stood over the body as Clay shared what little information he had gleaned from the two witnesses, approximate age, height, and possible race, wearing a black motorcycle jacket, and armed with a white stick or bat. Then together they divided up the workload to continue.

Doreen and Jimmy quickly headed around the immediate buildings and shops on the adjoining avenues to see if there were any cameras, Mark along with Officer Ortiz, from Patrol, began taking license plates from all of the parked cars on the block, and Clay and Tommy waited for the Crime Scene Unit and medical Examiner to arrive.

Crime Scene arrived shortly and quickly took their photos and measurements, then soon after Medical Examiner Kristen Smyth, arrived.

"Detective Keane, how are you tonight, sir?"

"Doing well, Smyth, how you doing this evening?" Tommy replied as he reached out and shook her small hand that poked out of a blue nylon parka that appeared to be two sizes too large for her little body.

Tommy liked ME Smyth, she was a tough, no-nonsense, medical examiner, but he still couldn't help thinking by her outward appearance that she would be more suited to be a suburban kindergarten teacher, rather than digging through dead bodies after visiting crime scenes at all hours of the day, but as with so many people, her first impression belied her abilities and professionalism.

"Busy as a little fucking bee tonight," Smyth replied.

"City hopping tonight?"

"Not so much the workload as the locations tonight, 6th precinct all the way to the 3-4, then back down to the 1st, now I'm here with you, and I have another waiting for me in the 3-0 I need to get to, so, uptown downtown, uptown downtown, plus we're shorthanded, but hey, that's how it goes some nights, so what do you have for me, sir?"

"First, let me introduce you to Clay Johnson, if you don't already know one another, this is his case tonight."

"Detective Johnson, nice to meet you, Kristen Smyth, Medical Examiner's office, what do you have for me tonight?"

"So nice to meet you, let me introduce you to Mr. Sol Abramowitz, who appears to have been hit several times until dead with a blunt object, but I will wait for your determination on that, Miss Smyth,"

Kristen Smyth stood over the body as she donned her latex gloves, then knelt next to Mr. Abramowitz' head, gently moving it to one side, a thick pool of dark read blood began to move toward her after she disturbed it until it found a crack in the sidewalk and began to follow its indentation.

"Yup, he's dead, and yes blunt force trauma, any idea what he was hit with? Do you have a weapon?"

"No, no weapon, but witnesses say it was a stick or a bat."

"Hmmm? I don't know, could be a stick, but at first look I'll say inconsistent, but regardless, it looks like he took three to four heavy blows with a hard heavy instrument of some kind, and that's what killed him – how about 4:00 pm tomorrow? I should be finishing up with his autopsy around then, does that work for you?"

"Uhh…" Clay paused for a moment, then looked at Tommy for a second, then replied, "Absolutely, I'll be there."

"Cool, here's my card, call me if you need anything."

Clay handed her his card, and they shook hands,

"Go ahead and give him a good going over now if you like, then my guys will bag and remove him… Gentlemen." She concluded with a nod, and with that ME Smyth was off to the next case.

Clay and Tommy began to give the body a thorough search, "Damn she's a cute tiny little thing, never peg her to crackin open chests in a morgue." Clay exclaimed.

"Right? Looks can be deceiving though, that little one is on top of her game." Tommy replied then gave the okay for the body to be removed, after which along with Mark, Doreen, and Jimmy, they then canvased the buildings on the block to see if they could find any new witnesses, or information pertinent to the investigation, unfortunately they did not.

Clay and Tommy then went to Mr. Abramowitz' apartment building, located at 300 East 71st Street. Upon arrival, the doorman informed the detectives that Mr. Abramowitz was a widower who lived alone, he knew he was a retired doctor but otherwise he was a quiet and kind old man who kept to himself. Clay attempted to get ahold of the super but was only able to leave a message, he also left a note with the doorman for the super to call him with any contact information for kin, and that he would return the next morning and may need to gain access to the apartment to continue with his investigation.

Chapter Three

12:52 AM

Once everyone returned to the Squad Room and regrouped, Lieutenant Bricks sat with the team as they discussed the case.

"So, any idea what happened to our victim?" Lieutenant Bricks began.

"No sir, not as of yet," Clay answered, then described the crime scene in full detail, "Although we have matching descriptions from our two eyewitnesses, they are pretty vague, I mean, outside of a white male twenty-five – thirty-five in a black motorcycle jacket, we have nothing, I do think, well I'm leaning towards the idea that the perp may have been known to our Vic?"

"Really? What makes you think that, Clay?"

"Well, Lu, it doesn't feel like a robbery to me, and the way the witnesses described the 'Fuck you's' the perp was spitting out, I just got the feeling that this was a more personal attack? … Like the perp knew the Vic, but I don't know, I'm just reaching?"

"No, that's reasonable, do we…"

"The one witness, I'm sorry, Lu, but the one witness described the perp as being confident, and, well again, I don't know where she got that from, but it makes me think these two, the perp and the Vic, may, possibly have been familiar, somehow, I don't know?"

"Okay, that's good, that's a little something, now do we, any of us think there is an antisemitic angle to this attack? We're all currently thinking it's not a robbery, correct?"

"Possibly a robbery gone wrong, Lu, but it looks like nothing was taken, so?" Doreen said.

"Cash in his front pocket, and a wallet full of credit cards in his back." Clay added.

"Okay, well hopefully it's not an antisemitic attack, and hopefully the media doesn't get wind of this and turn it into a press case, we certainly don't need that, and so far, we have nothing from any family?"

"No sir, Tommy and I went to his building over on 71st, but the old guy was a widower, and the doorman had nothing more to add, we're waiting on the Super to get back to us with some kind of family or emergency contact, but as of right now we got nothing."

"My computer search hasn't come up with anything worthwhile yet either, Lu," Doreen interjected, "Mr. Abramowitz, doesn't seem to have any social media profile, I found a little on his medical practice, he was a cardiologist, and it appears he retired about eight years ago, but so far nothing more than that."

"Well, that's to be expected I guess, given his age, I can imagine he may not be that active on social media, hell I've never had a social media account, and I'm almost twenty years younger than our Mr. Abramowitz here."

"Me neither, Lu, never had any interest," Tommy added.

"Yeah, but you're the 'Not quite adjusted 1950's guy' Tommy, your ass was born old!"

Jimmy and Doreen chuckled at Clay's statement.

"Seriously, I know this man for almost 20 years, the mans never played a video game, ain't that right?"

"True." Tommy replied.

"No Facebook, or Instagram, hell my man was the last man I know to make the leap from pager to cell phone, and that's because Lieutenant Shelby over in narcotics demanded he make the switch, ain't that right?"

"All true, I did try MySpace for about a half an hour when that was a thing, I thought it was the vapidest, most narcissistic place on the planet, so that didn't last, and I'm certain the rest of these platforms have only gotten worse."

"Ha, Mr. Man, on MySpace, I can't picture it, Tommy, creating his little profile, and making friends?" Said Doreen.

"Friends with who? Italian Village Pizza?" Jimmy chimed in.

"Alright, so as of now we have nothing more to discuss with this case, correct? Clay, you're satisfied at the moment and ready to pick it up tomorrow morning, yes? Tommy, you do a turnaround and come back tomorrow morning with Clay and hit this case hard, see if we can close it up quick."

"Yes, sir."

"And Tommy, you'll be secondary on this one, help Clay with anything he needs and get him familiar with the precinct, and really, well you know, help your friend out with anything he needs."

"Of course, Lu."

And with that everyone signed out for the evening and Tommy headed to his mother's on 88th Street, and Clay to his home in Yonkers.

***

Clarence "Clay" Johnson, at forty-four, was two years younger than Tommy. They attended the same police academy class but didn't know one another until they arrived to their FTU (Field Training Unit) in the 53rd Precinct in the Bronx, where they became fast friends.

Clay and Tommy went through FTU together, their time on patrol together, and served on the same Anti-Crime team together in the 5-3. Clay joined the Bronx Narcotics Division, approximately a year after Tommy had, and although they worked on different teams, they often saw one another in the office and occasionally worked together on buy and bust operations, or on larger cases which was a common occurrence in Narcotics when more manpower was needed than one team could provide.

About three years after Tommy left Narcotics and went to the 5-3 Squad, Clay left Narcotics to be assigned to the Special Victim's Unit for almost eight years before needing a change. That change landed him in the 2-1 where he found himself reunited with his old friend Tommy Keane.

Clay thought the world of Tommy, and the feeling was mutual. Both men loved and respected one another immensely and had a bond and a trust forged through adversity that few outside of cops and soldiers would understand.

Clay was born in Harlem, the eldest of three sons, his father also an NYPD Police Officer, and his mother a nurse, moved the family to Yonkers when Clay was 8.

Clay, who stood six foot four and a half, played high school football, and after graduation went on to play football at Saint John's University, where he studied computer programming. Numerous small injuries throughout his college career pulled the plug on football by his senior year, the same year he took his police exam.

The extremely affable and jovial Clay Johnson, just like his father, became a New York City Police Officer, married a nurse who worked at Jacobi Hospital, named Elsie Torrado, and had three beautiful boys. Clay and Elsie bought a house two blocks from the home Clay grew up in in Yonkers and enjoyed life and family to its fullest.

Chapter Four

Tommy and Clay signed in for their tour at the precinct then immediately headed down to 300 East 71st Street, Mr. Abramowitz' building to meet with the superintendent.

Built in 1960, 300 East 71st Street is a 19-story red brick building located on the corner of 71st Street and Second Avenue, and the building Dr. Abramowitz called home for almost fifty years.

Tommy and Clay pulled up and parked at the fire hydrant directly across the street from Dr. Abramowitz' building, then made their way across the street and into the lobby where they were met by a doorman, a young man of about 30, with a thin mustache named Hector.

Tommy immediately ID'd himself and showed his shield on his belt.

"Hey, how you doing? Detectives, Keane, and Johnson from the 21st Precinct, we're hoping to speak with the Super if he's available?"

"He said he would be, when he called me this morning." Clay added.

"Ha, I knew you two was cops as I watched you walk across the street and into the building, I knew it, I could tell by how yous walked, yeah just a minute please, let me call him."

Hector replied, then continued on a walkie talkie, "Hey, Jimmy, yeah it's Hector, I got two DTs here wanna talk to you, yeah man, sure," then turning his attention to the detectives, "He said he'll be right up, this about the Doctor, right? Abramowitz?"

"Yes sir it is, what can you tell us about him?" Tommy asked.

"Me? Well, not a whole lot, he was a very nice man, old man, I'm sure you know that he was a doctor, but he's been retired for as long as I can remember, lives alone, rarely any visitors, his wife has been passed for a long time now, I think I wanna say two kids, a son and a daughter, and they in their forties, I see them a few times a year, but not a whole lot… That's about it?"

As Hector finished his sentence, Jimmy Sherman, the super, a short, round, red-faced man, with a receding hairline and big smile dressed in a navy-blue Dickies uniform exited the elevator and made his way over to the detectives,

"Hello, Detective Johnson? Jimmy Sherman," he said as he extended his hand to Clay and then to Tommy, then repeating it as he took Tommy's hand, "Jimmy Sherman."

"How you doing? Detective Keane, 21st Precinct."

"No shit! I read about you in the paper all the time Detective Keane, nice to know you, wow, how about that Hector, this is the guy who saved those kids on Thanksgiving, and just broke the back of that Chinese mafia ring that was importing all those prostitutes and drugs from China, hell yeah, nice to know you, Detective."

"Well, thank you, Jimmy," Tommy sheepishly replied, slightly embarrassed by how excited Jimmy Sherman was to meet him.

"So, gentlemen, yous are in luck, I know you wanted to gain access to Dr. Sol's apartment, and I was worried I wouldn't have all the keys, but as it turns out, I checked and he didn't lock all three locks, just the door knob, so we'll be able to get in, also I spoke to the building manager, and he said no problem, just sign into our log book, and we'll be good to go!"

The detectives signed in and all three made their way up to the apartment on the 3rd floor.

"So, how well did you know Dr. Abramowitz?" Clay asked.

"I don't know. Not real well, I mean I have known him for the fifteen plus years I been workin' this building, but what can I say about Dr. Sol? Very nice man, never gives any of us a hard time, pretty generous around the holidays, struck me as a kind of a quiet lonely guy… he lost his wife some ten years ago, he's got a couple kids, the girl is very nice, the boy, not so much."

"Do you have their contact information?" Clay asked.

"I do in fact, here I prepared this for you this morning," Jimmy Sherman handed Clay an envelope, inside it was a sheet of paper with an itemized list printed on it, "It's a list of everything I could think of that you may ask me about the Doctor, hopefully this helps?"

"Well, thank you very much, Mr. Sherman, this will be very helpful sir. And this was very thoughtful also, man do I like a man who makes my life easier!"

Jimmy Sherman smiled and nodded, visibly happy with himself for making the list. "Hey, whatever you guys need."

Clay looked over the list, which included both kid's names and phone numbers, the address and a phone number to the doctors old office, a number to his old secretary, and a short description of the Doctors habits and routines which read:

1, A morning walk at 8:00 AM returning about 9:30 with the papers.

2, A trip to the Lenox Hill neighborhood Association at least three times a week, usually Mon, Wed & Fri, to swim.

3, An evening walk usually about 7-7:30 after dinner returning about 8-8:30 then he was in for the night.

4, Most Saturday mornings he would go to Temple at the Synagogue on 79th Street.

5, Dr. Abramowitz, was well-liked by the building's staff, was never a problem to anyone, and had lived in the building for about 50 years give or take.

After reading it over Clay looked up at Jimmy Sherman, "Thanks again, this is some good stuff." Then he and Tommy had a look around the apartment.

The place was neat, orderly, and nicely furnished, at first look you would never know Dr. Abramowitz was a widower, the apartment still had a feminine touch to it, with wedding and family photos on the walls, carefully placed lace doilies under each lamp, and under a candy dish full of hard ribbon candy on the coffee table made the place feel very homey, as if there were still a woman in the house.

As the detectives slowly moved from room to room searching for anything that may seem out of the ordinary, looking inside closets and drawers, the medicine cabinet, refrigerator, and kitchen cabinets, there was nothing they found that appeared odd or out of place to them, nothing that raised the slightest suspicion of these two veteran detectives, and so after about 45 minutes of nothing, both detectives once again thanked Jimmy Sherman for his help and left the building.

"Wasn't much there, was there?" Clay asked.

"No, nothing, but bless that Jimmy Sherman and that list, that will save us a little leg work."

"Yeah, no doubt, so, what next Tom, notify his kids I guess right?"

"Yeah, let's grab something to eat, make a couple of calls from the diner, see who we can possibly interview, and then head back to the precinct, for some computer searches if we need to?"

"Yes, sir, I like the way you think, let's get us to the diner, don't wanna be doing my searching on an empty stomach."

Chapter Five

9:12 AM

The Starlight Diner 1279 First Avenue

Tommy and Clay sat in a booth in the back of the restaurant, a very tired looking middle aged Greek woman in a white shirt and black pants approached and asked for the detective's order, "Good morning, how you doing today?" Tommy asked.

"Miserable, I am miserable today, thanks for asking."

"Miserable?" Clay asked, "What's got you down, honey?"

"Young people! Nobody wants to work anymore, all these young people, they want to make the money but not do the work for the money, you understand this? This is my tenth day working this week. I supposed to be off today but nobody come to work so here I am again, but forget about me, right now is for you, what you want, big man?"

"I'm sorry dear, I'll make it easy on you, just give me a bacon egg and cheese on a roll please, and a coffee." Clay answered,

"And you, not as big a man?"

Tommy smiled, "Give me a sausage, mushroom and American omelet, well done home fries and unsweetened iced tea, with whole wheat toast, please."

"You got it boys, give me a minute okay, we're short in the kitchen today too."

As the waitress walked away from the table Clay pulled out the list he received from the super and put in a call the Dr. Abramowitz' son David, and left a message, "Hello Mr. Abramowitz, Detective Johnson here from the 21st Precinct please return my call as soon as possible, thank you."

He then put in a call to his daughter Amanda, "Yes hello, I'm calling for Amanda Abramowitz, this is Detective Johnson from the 21st Precinct please call me back at your earliest convenience, thank you."

Less than a minute went by before Clay's phone went off, "Johnson" he answered.

"Yes, hello Detective Johnson, this is Amanda, Amanda Shellsburg, formerly Abramowitz, what can I do for you?"

"Hello Mrs. Shellsburg, I'm calling about your father, I'm very sorry to inform you that he passed last night, I would like, if possible, come and see you this morning to discuss the circumstances and…"

"Oh, my, God! Why yes, oh my God, yes, what happened to my father, was, was it not natural causes?"

"No, no ma'am it wasn't I'm sorry to say, is it possible, can you tell me where you are, and I'll come visit you and explain?"

"Yes, of course, I, you can come to my office, I'm at Jonas & Jonas Real Estate, 199 East 85th Street suite B."

"And what time will work for you today?"

"Oh, gee, can you give me an hour? I'll, I'll be ready in an hour, is that okay?"

"That's absolutely okay Mrs. Shellsburg, I'll see you then."

"How'd she take it?" Tommy asked.

"Sounded shocked, she'll be ready for us in an hour, so plenty of time to eat then head up to 85th."

***

10:16 AM

The office of Jonas & Jonas Real Estate

Tommy and Clay entered suite B of 199 East 85th Street, a nicely appointed, but fairly generic, office with grey carpets and grey walls adorned with large photos of high-rise buildings, their windows glistening in the sun against blue skies. A very attractive olive-skinned woman with jet black hair of about twenty-four sat behind a black marble-topped receptionist station. She immediately asked. "Good morning, how may I help you gentlemen?"

"Detective Johnson, 21st Precinct, here to see Amanda Shellsburg please."

"Oh my god, yes," she said in a half whisper, "you're here about her father, my god I'm so sorry, yes please come this way."

She stood and walked the detectives two doors down a hallway to a meeting room with a large table surrounded by eight chairs.

"Here sit, I'll get her for you right away."

Both Detectives took a seat at the table only to immediately stand back up as Jessica entered the room.

"Detective Johnson?" Amanda asked through welled up eyes as she reached her hand out to take Clay's hand.

"Yes, ma'am, and this here is my partner Detective Keane, please Mrs. Shellsburg, sit down and I'll explain the situation surrounding your fathers passing."

As the three sat at the table, Amanda asked, "My brother David is on his way, we spoke right after your call and I told him you would be meeting me here, would you like to wait for him to arrive, he shouldn't be much longer?"

"Would you prefer we wait ma'am; would you like him here for support? I want you to be comfortable?"

"Actually no, I, I'm too nervous to wait, please tell me what happened, what happened to my father, and please Detective, call me Amanda?"

"Okay, Amanda, your father, was attacked last night, he was struck in the head several times with a hard object, and sadly he passed away because of his injuries," A look of horror and confusion came across Amanda's face, as Clay continued, "At the moment we don't know much else, we have a vague description of his assailant we received from two witnesses, we're not sure if this was a robbery attempt or just an outright assault, but…"

Just then there was a knock at the door and Amanda's brother David cracked open the door and stuck his head in then fully opened it and stepped in.

"Hello, I'm David Abramowitz."

Both Detectives stood up and greeted David.

"I'm Detective Johnson from the 21st precinct, and this is my partner Detective Keane, please sir sit down."

Clay then repeated the information he had given to Amanda to David.

"So, you guys have nothing concerning my father's death as of yet?" David asked in a surprising matter of fact manner, his face showing no signs of emotion at all.

"No, sir, not at the moment, but being here is part of that, what we'll need from the two of you is a little personal information, and then for one or both of you to identify the body."

"What personal information could you possibly need from either of us? Certainly, you're not suggesting that either of…"

"David!" Amanda abruptly cut David off in a firm and objectionable tone, "These men are here to assist us in finding out who in this city has murdered our father, please do not make this conversation about you, or any ridiculous agenda you are propagating this month, these men are on our side."

David froze for a moment, then in a softer, more somber tone he began again "Amanda, you're right and I am sorry, I'm just very, very stressed, I'm sure these officers understand, this is shocking news, and you know how poorly I handle stressful situations, and the thought of them accusing you or I…"

"David!... enough." Then directing her gaze from the table to Clay's eyes, "Please, Detective, go ahead and ask any questions you may have, and I will go to identify the body whenever you need me to."

"Amanda, I can go with…"

"David… I will take care of the identification, and I'll do it alone, or with Michael… Detective Johnson, please go ahead."

The room hung in silence for just a moment, Amanda's eyes now focused back on the table as were David's. Tommy and Clay's eyes bounced glances between one another and the two siblings trying to figure out this obviously strange relationship.

"Okay, all I'll really need from the two of you at the moment is to know each of your whereabouts yesterday at approximately 8:00 PM, David would you like to start?"

David began in a low sheepishly subdued tone, "Yes, sir, at 8PM I was home, with my wife, her name is Rachel, she can absolutely confirm that, and so can my doorman, I arrived home at about 6:30 and never left the house again, my doorman Stu, will confirm that, and my wife Rachel can confirm I didn't leave the house again until this morning."

"Okay great, thank you David, and you Amanda, where were you at about 8:00 PM last night?"

"I would have just about been getting home about that time Detective Johnson, and my husband Michael, and my daughter Jenna, can confirm that, and I assume my doorman

Walter can also attest to my arrival at about 8:00 PM, usually I leave here at 6:00 and head straight home but last night I had my nails done over at Little Paint nails on Third Avenue, and therefore I got home a little later."

"Okay great, so we know where you were, now do either of you think there is anyone who would wish harm on your father, for any reason whatsoever?"

"No, my father was loved by everyone who ever met him." Amanda immediately replied.

"David?" Clay asked.

"Amanda, you're in the real estate world, do you think that Father's landlord could be involved?"

Amanda looked into her brother eyes, "Don't be preposterous, David, of course not."

"Well, he did live there for fifty years, and his rent was so so low, do you think we'll be able to keep the apartment Amanda, I mean if I wanted a suspect I would…"

"David! … Stop it now, this is serious business, I can't believe you're asking about the apartment," then exasperated and stressed, "Detective Johnson, is it possible we end this meeting now? Do you need more from us at the moment? Let me know when and where to identify my father and I will be there, and if you have any follow-up inquiries at all I will be more than willing to cooperate with you to my fullest, but, but at the moment, if you are thinking we can I would like to end this meeting, and go back to work."

Clay glanced at Tommy quickly, and not seeing anything positive or negative in Tommy's eyes, Clay responded in a very kind and concerned tone.

"Mrs. Shellsburg, we can absolutely finish this interview now if you are feeling stressed, and have work to do, I understand this is a lot to take in, believe me I do, you have my number from earlier I assume, but here is my card as well, as far as the identification of your father you can do that anytime…"

"And we can escort you to the morgue and bring you back home and or here to the office if you like, Amanda." Tommy interrupted, "Sorry, Clay, go ahead."

"Would you prefer that, Amanda? We can bring you back and forth if that helps at all?" Clay added.

"Yes, I think that's best."

Tommy wrote the address and phone number of the morgue on the back of his card and handed it to Amanda, "Here is the information you'll need if you choose to go on your own, but just call Clay, and we'll be happy to bring you down."

"Thank you, thank you both so much, how, how soon can I, should I go?"

"We can take you today, or tomorrow if that's more convenient?"

"Oh my god, Yes, well… today, let's do it today please."

David again tried to speak up, but Amanda put up her hand and said "No" to whatever he was about to propose, "I want to go alone David, you go home and be with Rachel, I'll call you tonight." Then redirecting her attention back to Clay, "Let me make arrangements here please, I should be able to leave in less than an hour if that works for you, if not maybe later this afternoon?"

"Less than an hour is absolutely doable if that's what works for you?" Tommy replied.

"Okay then, I'll call you in 20-30 minutes to confirm my availability."

"Very good," Tommy stood and shook Amanda's hand then shook David's hand, "We are truly sorry for your loss."

Clay did the same, "Yes, we are sorry, the little we know about your father says he was a very decent man."

And with that, they left the office suite and headed to the elevator, as they did, they could hear "David enough!" one more time before saying goodbye to the receptionist and stepping into the hallway.

Clay could see the elevator door closing and ran to catch it, but Tommy said, "No, Clay, let it go," then explained, "Give it a minute, we'll see if our David follows us out, we'll see what this character has to say on the ride down, maybe even offer him a ride home?"

"Tommy, you slick ass bastard, I like it! Nice to be working with you again, Two Gun." Clay grinned.

"You keep calling me that and this will be the last day big man."

And just as Tommy predicted as they stood in the hallway talking nonsense, David Abramowitz stepped into the hallway and joined them in front of the elevator.

"Let me apologize, Detectives. I have some authority issues, and I can be a bit neurodivergent at times, my sister explained to me how you guys are on our side, and I want to let you know I support you in this investigation and the police as a whole with everything you do."

"Well, thank you, David, we really appreciate that, and please know sir, we absolutely are on your side and are determined to find out what happened to your father," Tommy said then followed up with, "Where are you headed sir, can we give you a lift?"

"A ride, home? I'd appreciate that, thanks, if it's not out of the way?"

"We can do that, no trouble at all, especially after the day you've had." Clay said as all three men stepped into the elevator, then Tommy began.

"I know this has been an exceptionally stressful morning for you and your sister, David, and again we are so sorry for your loss, but I have to ask, man to man, if I'm not getting too personal or prying, what is up with your sister and constantly cutting you off?"

"My sister, well my sister has control issues, she thinks she is the smartest thing and knows better than everyone else, and well I, I just play along with her, it's so much easier than the constant confrontation, and I see how you two might think she was emasculating me up there, but I've learned it is so much easier to just let her rant you know?"

"Yes, I think I can see what you're saying, Tommy replied, but we would really like to hear what you had to say, and it just seemed every time you had something to add Jessica just shot you down and cut you off before you could get anything off your chest."

The three men stepped out of the building and walked toward the car as the conversation continued.

"Oh my god I know, she can be so rude sometimes, I'm glad you noticed, Detective, she is not the easiest person to deal with, not by a long shot."

"Where to David, 63rd you said?"

"Yes 63rd and Lex would be great, thank you."

"And now that it's just the three of us, what are your thoughts on your father's death?"

"Well, I wanted to make the point that my father pays less than a thousand dollars a month to live in that apartment, and I have heard of landlords killing off tenants to get their apartments back."

"It happens, no doubt." Said Clay

"And my father's place, well really our place, my sister and I lived there our entire lives until we were married as well, is an absolute gem of an apartment, you should see it." Clay and Tommy stayed silent, "I know a lot of people would kill for such a place, especially for the rent he's paying, my god it's an absolute steal."

"So, you are thinking someone killed your father for his apartment?" Clay asked.

"I'm saying it's possible the landlord wanted it back, and especially before my sister or I moved back in, you know if we were still living there the place would be ours for life, they'd never get rid of us, then I'd be the eighty-year-old man paying less than a thousand dollars a month for that fabulous apartment… Hey, you guys know the law right, do you think we could still claim the apartment as our own legally, you know even though we have been out of there for years now?"

"Sorry, David, that's not a police issue, it's a civil issue, so different laws apply, laws that we the police aren't apprised of." Tommy said. "Let me ask you, David, what is it you and your wife Rachel do for work?"

"We're both freelance creators. I build and create video games, a lot of virtual reality stuff, and my wife creates content on TikTok and Instagram."

"Really! Wow that sounds exciting, how long have you been doing that?" Clay asked.

"About twenty-four years now, ever since college."

"Have you worked on anything I may know, I'm a bit of a gamer myself?"

David paused and stared out the window, "Unlikely, most of my stuff is for the European markets, much more artsy and experimental, it's an entirely different world than what you find here in America."

"63rd and Lexington," Tommy announced as he pulled the car over to curb, "If you think of anything else concerning your father, please give us a call sir."

"Yes, I will." David said as he exited the vehicle without a thank you or a goodbye.

Both detectives sat silently for a moment as they watched David walk up the block.

"That little full of shit lying motherfucker, fuck his ass and his selfish lying mouth!" Clay couldn't hold back.

"Ha! So, tell me what you think?"

"What I think, I'll tell you what I think, I think this selfish mother fucker doesn't care one bit that some piece of shit crushed his daddy's skull, and it's most definitely obvious he wants to move him and his bullshit TikTok creating wife back into his daddy's apartment, now that he's been put down for the dirt nap, that's what I think!"

"So, you liking him for this?"

Clay paused, took a breath, then took a second breath, "Nah… I wish it would turn out to be him, but I ain't feelin' it. I'm gonna check out his alibi for sure, but no, I don't think this kid has it in him, but hey, you never know right? What you think, you feelin' anything about this loser?"

"Not at the moment. I'm in the same boat as you, I don't think he's our man, not as the actor, and he doesn't seem like a guy to hire someone, that being said you never know, and we'll have to see where this investigation leads, let's go pick up Amanda, for the ID, maybe we'll get more from her about her brother, and herself?"

"You think she could be involved somehow?"

"I'm not liking her for this one bit at the moment, but again, you never know."

Chapter Six

After dropping off David, Tommy and Clay returned to 199 East 85th Street to pick up Amanda. As Tommy parked the car, Clay called the office to let her know they were waiting downstairs, Tommy then called the morgue to let them know they would be bringing Amanda Shellsburg down to identify her father.

They discussed how they would approach, and conversate with Amanda on their way to and from the morgue, neither believed she was involved in any way in her father's death, but both also knew it was often easier to extract information via conversation than questioning, so both agreed to just keep the conversation light, and see where it would lead.

Both detectives then stepped out of the vehicle and leaned against it as they stood on the sidewalk and waited for Amanda to arrive, which she did in a matter of minutes. As she approached it was obvious she had pulled herself together and was in a better state of mind.

Everyone said hello as Amanda approached the car, and Clay opened the door for her as Tommy made his way around to the driver's side.

Tommy gave a brief description of what Amanda should expect from the experience and promised it would literally be less than a minute once they arrived and signed in.

After that discussion, Clay said they would drive her home afterward just as they had David.

"Oh my god, you guys drove him home? I'm sorry, I hope he didn't go off on any political rants while he was with you."

"No ma'am, he was for the most part a perfect gentleman," Clay responded, "Should we have expected a rant?"

"Listen, I know when we were upstairs, in my office the situation was a bit tense, but gee what can I say, my brother, my brother is really a very intentionally difficult asshole at times."

Tommy looked in the rearview mirror at her, trying not to smile, "Is that part of his neurodivergence?"

"Ugh, he told you that? No, my brother is not mentally ill, but what he is, is a selfish narcissist who has never done a day of work in his life, and lives off of the trust fund my parents invested in for each of us so we could live well and hopefully do well for our children… He is not neurodivergent, does not have Aspergers, or any other sort of spectrum-related autism or affliction he or his idiot girlfriend deem interesting this month."

"Girlfriend? Is Rachel not his wife?" Clay asked.

"No, they have lived together for over ten years now, but no, never have either of them been married, not to each other or to anyone else, she, like my brother, is an over-educated fool who spent eight years in college and university, to have no degree, and who also relies on her parent's money for survival, sadly neither are contributing members to society,"

Amanda took a deep breath as her eyes welled up with tears, "And you heard him… Did you? Did you hear him, not one ounce of concern for my father, not a bit, but right away he wants to know if he can move into that apartment, my god, my god, my god … I just don't understand."

She paused again and the car went silent, then she began to apologize,

"I'm so sorry, Detectives," she said through tears and sniffles, "I know you don't need to hear this and you just have a job to do. I'm sorry, my brother David has just been such a burden and such a worry for us. My mother and father loved him so, but never, never would he put forth any effort in school or in life, when I got out of law school my mother was dealing with her first bout of cancer when she made me promise to take care of David, believing he had special needs."

"But he had none?" Clay asked.

"No, of course not, in fact, he was an absolutely normal kid until he got into college and realized he could play video games and smoke pot through school, and not put in any effort as long as he had an excuse or disability. In high school, he was an A student, then in college he somehow developed dyslexia, then Asperger syndrome, that was a big hit for him, he learned all about it… then simply recited every symptom to any doctor, or counselor that was in front of him, and that was it, he discovered and mastered the game of getting over on the system… it doesn't work on me though, my father saw through it too, but he went along to appease my mother."

"I'm sorry dear, sounds like a lot to deal with?" Tommy asked.

"My poor mother, she loved him so much."

Tommy parked the car in front of the entrance, and the three entered the building, met with the receptionist, and signed in. Tommy and Clay then walked Amanda Shellsburg to a glass window where a stainless-steel table sat on the other side, with the obvious outline of a body under a cover. Tommy asked Amanda if she was ready and she said yes, and he nodded yes to the gentleman behind the glass who pulled the cover down just enough to expose a man's face.

Amanda let out a soft gasp, looking at the pale gaunt face of her dead father, his eyes staring straight up at the ceiling and his mouth slightly open, the man she knew and loved her entire life, was now gone, lying lifeless on a cold stainless-steel table.

She said, "Yes, that is my father."

Tommy nodded again and the man behind the glass re-covered the man's face, and Tommy and Clay escorted Amanda back outside onto the sidewalk and to the car.

She visibly straightened her spine, took a deep breath of the cool air, wiped tears from both of her eyes, then looking at both Tommy and Clay, said-

"Thank you, Detectives, thank you for driving me over, and for being here with me. Please catch whoever did this to my father, he was a good, good man, and did not deserve to die this way." Both Tommy and Clay pursed their lips and bowed their heads slightly, "There's no need to drive me home, I think a long walk in this cool air will do me good and give me time to take in the day, my god, just a few hours ago I was giving breakfast to my daughter before she left for school and my husband left for work, what a strange day."

And with that she walked away, Tommy and Clay stood and watched until she was out of site, Clay still looking in Amanda's direction, "Strange day indeed."

***

"We are very early, but what say we check in with ME Smyth and see if she can tell us anything while we are here?" Tommy asked Clay.

"Makes sense, we here ain't we?"

After re-entering through the reception area, they headed into the room where the autopsies were done.

"Man, I hate this place, haven't been here for years." Clay stated, halfway holding his breath from the foul odor of death.

"You'll get used to it." Tommy replied.

"Shiiiit, I hope I never do."

"Good afternoon, Detective Keane, Detective Johnson, how are you gentlemen today?" Kristen Smyth asked, "You guys actually interrupted my autopsy of Mr. Abramowitz, with your victims ID."

"Not too bad, Smyth, my friend Clay is not thrilled to be here, though, not a lot of autopsies in narcotics or special victims, but otherwise I'm doing very well thanks. And, yes, I'm sorry we're here early today but it turned out to be the most opportune time for the victim's daughter."

"No problem, I get it, and are you feeling alright Detective Johnson?"

"Yeah, I feel fine, It's, well it's just been years since I've been here, and well, let's just say I don't care for the atmosphere." he said, as he turned his head and looked over the three separate corpses that lay on stainless steel tables, and made a bit of a wincing face obviously relating to the smell of the room.

"Ahh, I see and understand, but you'll get used to it."

Tommy smiled.

"I hope not." Clay replied.

"Okay, so not a lot to this one, our victim Mr. Abramowitz, was killed by being struck what appears to be four times in the head with a blunt object. It was these blows that killed him … not hitting his heard on the sidewalk, I believe, or it appears to me he first went to his knees in the fall and then from there became completely prone causing only this minor abrasion here to his head, and the rest of these wounds were caused by whatever he was struck with?"

"Do you think with was a stick or a bat?" asked Tommy.

"Neither. These wounds are all consistent with one another, however they are all oddly shaped, with a strange angular impression and depth that is not consistent with anything I personally have seen before. Now whatever, and whoever, caused them wielded a considerable amount of force, enough to break through our victim's skull with two of the four blows it appears he took."

"So, we're looking at a particularly strong assailant?" asked Clay.

"Yes, I would say definitely a strong assailant, or a weapon with some sort of accelerant, maybe like a flail, or a set of nunchakus, you know the Japanese weapon, with the two sticks and a chain."

"Interesting, so you think our man used nu chucks?"

"Actually no, I don't, again the wounds are not consistent with the end of a wooden stick, or club, they have a strange shape, and angle to them, and although they are consistent to one another, they are not consistent in shape or depth to anything I have witnessed before. My nunchakus remark was that I think it is possible that our assailant's weapon may have had a way to gain momentum and power to cause such devastating injuries, possibly something like nunchakus, or a medieval flail, the chain or rope, increasing the force of the blow beyond that of the individual swinging the weapon."

"Right, I got you, now I understand," Clay responded.

"Other than that, I don't have much else for you gentlemen today. Our Mr. Abramowitz here was in excellent physical condition especially for his age, and I would imagine he had many years left, I have a preliminary report here for you but it will be a few days before the labs and toxicology come back and I submit my final, but regardless I really think I have told you everything you're going to need for this one, good luck fellas!"

Tommy and Clay said goodbye and headed back to the car. "Lunch?" Tommy asked.

"Lunch!" Clay replied.

"So, the morgue hasn't slowed your appetite?"

"Shit, we ain't eating in the morgue, are we?"

Chapter Seven

3:44 PM

Blockheads Burrito restaurant, 954 2nd Avenue

On the way back to the 2-1, Tommy and Clay stopped to grab a bite at Blockhead Burrito on 2nd Avenue and 51st Street. A very cute little Mexican joint that was one of Tommy's favorite lunch stops in the city and had recently rediscovered with Jimmy Coletti during the Jenny Black case.

Tommy had a grilled steak burrito, and Clay a chicken quesadilla.

"Who woulda thought man, almost twenty years ago we met each other in FTU, up in the 5-3, now here we are chasing killers together in Manhattan?" Clay asked Tommy, as they munched on some corn chips and salsa as they waited for their meals to arrive.

"I don't know where the time went. Seems just like yesterday we were standing on a foot post on 194th Street together, when you got hit with a diaper some asshole threw out a window at you."

"Really? All our times together, that's the moment you gonna bring up, me with all that stanky mustard green baby poo all down my uniform, and all them civilians laughing at me, that's the story you wanna remember and bring up, here while we eating a nice lunch and reminiscing about days gone by. Okay for you, I'll remember that next time I got some stories to tell up in the squad, I'll do my best to pull up some embarrassing shit on your ass." Clay replied with a laugh and a smile, "Damn, that was some rank smellin' poo though, I remember that!"

As the two continued to reminisce, Clay's phone went off; "Johnson… Oh hey, Charice, how you doing honey? Oh yeah? Cool, we be back in less than an hour and I'll look into it, thank you, yes ma'am, thank you."

"Charice? What's up?" Tommy asked.

"Yeah, that was Charice, she just got into work and said a tip came into the 777 line for me about this case, woo hoo! We might have ourselves a lead, be nice to close my first big 2-1 case up within the first 48!"

"Let's hope it's a good one!" Tommy said as he lifted his glass in a salute to good luck and a quick apprehension.

***

4:54 PM

2-1 Precinct

Tommy and Clay made their way to the squad room, and Charice, who was on the phone, raised her index finger to the detectives to indicate she needed a minute, both men paused a moment and waited for her to finish her conversation.

"Okay you two, give me a second, where is it?" She stated, after hanging up the phone, "Here you go, Detective

Johnson, here is your tip info from the 777-TIPS hot line, I hope it's fruitful!"

"Thank you, Charice, I appreciate this."

"And you, Detective Keane, let me say it again, I am so happy to see you back here where you belong! We missed you, Tommy! We missed you terribly, especially Doreen, she was very worried about you, so you make sure to give her a little extra attention, okay?"

"Yes ma'am, I will, and it's good to be back Charice, and so good to see that beautiful smile of yours again, I myself missed that each day."

"I bet you did!" Charice replied loudly with a wink and a smile.

As Tommy and Clay had done a turn-around from the previous evening, their squad was still on its regular schedule and they had all just made it in to begin their shifts, so all the greetings went around the office, to Mark Stein, Doreen Doyle, Jimmy Coletti, and Sergeant Browne who was at the time complaining about the cleanliness of the squad rooms refrigerator.

"Is that Keane and Johnson?" Lieutenant Bricks shouted from his office.

"Yes Lu, it's us!" Clay shouted back.

"Come on in here and tell me what you got."

Tommy and Clay entered Lieutenant Brick's office.

"Sit down men, tell me where we're at with this Abramowitz case, we find anything out today?"

Clay began, "It's been an interesting day, Lu, autopsy says he was killed by blunt force trauma, no surprise there. We interviewed the superintendent, did a walk-through of the deceased's apartment, nothing unusual there, interviewed the deceased's son and daughter, that was interesting."

"Interesting how?"

"They were both kinda odd. The son David was out right squirrelly, definitely some personality flaws bordering on mental illness with him, and the daughter, well she was heartbroken, that was obvious, but also had some control issues with the brother, who seemed to be more worried about his father's apartment, than his father's death, whole thing was odd."

"Do you think either of these two are involved with this homicide?"

"I'm not feeling nothing of the sort for the daughter, Lu, but the boy, like I said he's squirrely, I ain't gonna say I'm liking him just yet, but I am gonna say I'm going to look a little deeper."

"And your thoughts, Tom?"

"I'm right there with Clay, at the moment we have nothing, no evidence pointing towards either of these two, my only buts are, he is definitely off mentally, which the sister confirmed, and then the strange dynamic between them, she kept him on a very short leash while we were all together, he again seemed more concerned about their fathers apartment than his death, and in that same respect, she is a lawyer who works for a large real estate company… right now it's all nothing, a bit suspicious maybe, but again, as of right now we got nothing but… Tell him Clay."

"Yes, tell me Clay."

"A tip just came in from 777-TIPS, So, we may have ourselves a lead!"

"Well, what the hell you in here talking to me for? Go check out that lead!"

***

Tommy and Clay sat across from one another at Detective Volpe, and Keogh's desks, and took a look at the TIPS sheet that they had just received from Charice.

Clay read it aloud, "Name, phone number, and address of a Mr. Joel Friedleman, says he knows who killed the old man on 66th Street… looks like he lives just a couple blocks down from where the killing took place."

"Awesome!" Tommy replied, "Let's run our Mr. Friedleman in the system and see what we can find out about him, then give him a call and see if we can interview him today?"

"Hells yeah, I'm on it!" Clay excitedly stated as he began typing away on the computer.

"Friedleman?" Doreen asked from her desk, "I think I know that name, does that sound familiar to either of you?" Nodding her head towards Mark and Jimmy.

"Means nothing to me." Jimmy replied, not removing his eyes from his keyboard as he typed away on one of his current cases.

"Yes," Stien replied as he put a cup of coffee to his lips and took a sip and starred off into nothingness trying to remember why that name was familiar… "Volpe," was his initial one-word answer, then a pause as he again thought for a second. "Volpe had a case, a similar assault actually, happened over the summer, maybe July or August before you were assigned here, Tom, very similar circumstances, almost identical now that I think about it … older Jewish man, hit in the head with a hard object, no homicide though, just minor injuries, that was Volpe's case, if I remember correctly, Friedleman's name was attached, I think he was interviewed as a witness or something, nothing came of the case I think, old guy recovered just fine, and I don't believe there was ever an arrest? Ask the Lu, he may know?"

Tommy and Clay made their way across the Squad Room and stepped into Lieutenant Bricks' office, "Hey, Lu, do you remember an assault that Volpe had over the summer, older Jewish fella hit over the head, minor injuries? Any idea if there was an arrest, or can you remember any specifics?"

"Yeah, Tom, I remember that case, and no, there never was an arrest on that one, nothing much to go on, only witness turned out not to be a witness at all if I remember correctly, just some crackpot who said he knew the attacker, but nothing ever panned out."

"Any idea on the name of that crackpot, Lu?" Clay asked.

"Hmm? No nothing comes to mind, but it will be in Volpe's case folder, take a…"

"Friedleman?" Clay interrupted.

"Now that rings a bell, Clay… Friedleman? That sounds correct, let me guess, he's the man calling in the tip, yes?"

"Yes, sir, that's the man."

"Well, go ahead and do the right thing and go take his statement, get with Volpe too, he may have some insight, or something in that old case folder that may help you out… good luck."

"Thanks Lu."

They headed back to the desks and as they did Tommy put in a call to Volpe."

"Hey, Tom, what can I do for you?" Was how he answered the phone.

"Hey, man, Clay and I are on speaker phone here, Clay caught a homicide, I'm sure you heard, well it may be connected to an assault you had over the summer, older Jewish fella, hit in the head…"

"Yeah Harry Greenblatt, nice old guy, odd case, cracked in the head from behind, no witnesses, evidence or leads, ended up going nowhere, luckily only minor injuries."

"You had a tip though right? Clay asked.

"Yeah, some nut job, guy named Joel Friedleman, called in saying he knew who the killer was, called in on the 777-TIPS line. Keogh and I interviewed him, he was an obvious crazy, Sergeant Ruffalo told me he was a chronic caller when he heard I interviewed him, skinny nervous kid, mid to late twenties, lives on 63rd with an equally crazy mother… Odd thing though, nothing he said panned out, or even came off as true, but he did know about the assault, kept calling it a murder, and saying a guy named Stanley was responsible for the murder, but we couldn't find this Stanley, or corroborate anything else Friedleman told us, and of course there was no murder, just three stitches in old man Greenblatt's chin from where he hit the sidewalk… Go ahead and check out the case folder, it's in the files under Greenblatt."

"Hey thanks man, I appreciate it."

"No problem, hit me back if you need anything else."

Tommy stood and went over to the filing cabinets and retrieved the case folder as Clay searched out Joel Friedleman on the department's computer system.

Tommy found nothing of value within the folder, jotted down Mr. Greenblatt's contact information and then placed the folder on the desk where Clay continued his computer searches.

"Not much here, Clay, all the times, dates, and interviews, but nothing that points us toward anything, only person in this folder who had anything to say at all was Friedleman, who it is noted here just continued to say that an unknown Stanely, was responsible for a murder that didn't happen, and Volpe searched for a Stanely, but nothing came of it, it states here that he found Friedleman to be an unreliable chronic caller."

"Ahh! So, it's looking like this 777-TIPS ain't gonna be the godsend I was hoping for, would have liked my first 2-1 homicide to be open and shut, and impress the Lu and the captain, but now I'm thinking this ain't gonna be an easy one?"

"Nothing ever is down here, when I was in the 5-3, I was catching 10-15 homicides a year myself, but half of them were drug related and we had the perps in cuffs within the week, the other half was gang or domestic shit and we usually closed those within a week as well, down here we're working an eighth of the crime we had in the 5-3, but none of these cases are ever cut and dry, it's always some convoluted Agatha Christie who dunnit shit."

"Yeah, I can see that, let me call this Friedleman, see if we can get with him tonight?"

"Hey man you never know. It sounds unlikely, but he may shed some light on this one?"

- 72 -

Chapter Eight

6:46 PM

427 East 63rd Street Apartment 1C

Tommy and Clay arrived at the apartment of Joel Friedleman and were greeted at the door by a short, very thin, woman with a cigarette hanging from her mouth. She wore a simple house dress, with a blue flowered print, and dingy cream-colored slippers. Joel's mother, Mrs. Edna Friedleman, was fifty-seven years old, but her unkempt salt and pepper hair, thickly framed glasses, and thin, frail build, made her appear closer to seventy.

She spoke slowly, in a gravely yet rather high-pitched voice, and a heavy New York accent. "Hello, hello Detectives, and welcome, welcome to our humble home, my Joel told me you'd be visiting, come, come on in and have a seat, here on the sofa, he'll be right back."

"Thank you, ma'am," Clay said as he stepped inside, "I'm Detective Johnson, and this is my partner Detective Keane."

"Edna, pleasure to know you, I'm sure. Can I get you gentleman some coffee? Joel will be right back; he went to get some Entenmann's for us."

"No, thank you dear, we're on a tight schedule tonight, and were just hoping to speak to Joel for a moment." Clay replied, "So he's not here you're saying?"

"He will be in just a minute, he's excited to meet with you and wanted to have some Entenmann's when you arrived."

As Clay and Edna spoke, Tommy's eyes scanned the room. The apartment was clean and tidy and smelled of cigarettes. The furnishings all appeared to be well over forty years old, however, everything appeared to be well taken care of and in order.

"Is it just you and your son living here at the moment, Mrs. Friedleman?" Clay asked.

"Edna please, yes, it's just been me and my Joel for the last fourteen years. This was actually my parent's apartment, I grew up here in this apartment until I got married to my husband at twenty-six, but when he passed … my Joel was only a baby, just a year old … we moved back in here with my father. He passed about fourteen years ago, and since then it's been just me and my Joel."

"I'm sorry for your losses, Edna, must be tough raising a boy on your own?"

"Ahh, we do what we have to, the state takes good care of us with the disability, and we have the rent control, so we aren't going anywhere anytime soon." Edna said with a smile, "and I had my poppa help me with Joel until he was twelve, he passed just before we could bar mitzvah my Joel, that was a bit of a blow, but we do alright my Joel and I."

"Sounds like you have a solid relationship. Tell me a little bit about Joel, where does he work?"

"Oh, he's a fine boy, he takes good care of me, does a lot of the shopping for me, helps around the apartment, very sweet boy. He doesn't work anymore, he's got a bit of a nervous condition, you know … what they call on the anxiety, but he's a fine, fine boy, and yes, we get along very well here, we're both on disability from the state."

"I see," Tommy interjected, "Does Joel get out much, or is he more of a home body?"

"He gets out, more than I do, like I said, he does a lot of the shopping for me now, and he'll meet up with friends once or twice a week, he plays video games here with his friends and they meet up for pizza once or twice a week?"

"That's nice to hear, so his friends come here to the apartment to play video games?"

"Oh no, no, I'm too nervous to have a bunch of boys running around my apartment. They all play games together online, you know how they play those war games, sometimes with teams, I don't understand it, but gaming is what all the young people do these days."

"Yes ma'am, I'm a bit of a gamer myself." Clay replied.

As they spoke the door opened and in stepped Joel. Joel stood at about six feet tall, he had a stringy, moppy head of hair that almost made it to his shoulders. He wore a grey wool pea coat over an oversized navy sweater, wrinkled blue jeans, and beat-up New Balance sneakers. His entire appearance screamed of a pseudo intellectual gamer, who at twenty-six, still lived at home with his mother, and it suited him because that's exactly what he was.

With a big smile and an eager, almost excited, attitude he greeted the detectives,

"Hello, hello, I'm Joel, happy, very happy to meet you gentlemen, you detective gentlemen." Joel spoke awkwardly, trying to appear formal and in control of himself, yet the inner child in him shone through as if he were meeting a sports hero or celebrity.

"I bought some Entenman's, I didn't know what you gentlemen detectives would like so I got Louisiana Crunch Cake, Raspberry Danish Twist, and some chocolate chip cookies, because who doesn't like chocolate chip cookies? Am I right?"

"I'm sorry Joel, but these men are on a tight schedule tonight, and they can't stay for coffee dear." Edna stated rather flatly.

Joel's face went from one of joy to disappointment, and as he nervously began to speak, "Oh, okay, I just wanted…"

Tommy said, "I could certainly go for some coffee, Edna, and maybe two of those cookies. I mean, who doesn't like chocolate chip cookies, am I right, Joel?"

Joel's face lit up again, "Yes sir!"

Clay, realizing that Joel was a bit off, nodded to Tommy in approval, "I'll have four of those cookies with my coffee please, Joel."

"Okay then," Edna began, also with a bit of happiness in her voice, "You men have a seat on the sofa with my Joel and ask him about what you came here to ask him, and I'll bring out the coffee and the Entenmann's."

Tommy, Clay, and Joel all took their seats in the living room, and Clay began.

"So, you called 777-TIPS about an attack that happened two nights ago, Joel, what do you know?"

Joel took a deep breath, his demeanor going from overjoyed to almost solemn, he lowered his head slightly and said, "It was Stanley who did it, he killed that man on 66th Street."

"And you're sure of this?"

"Absolutely, 100%"

"And how do you know, did you see the attack?"

"No, he, Stanley told me about it."

"Okay, and who is Stanley to you?"

"A friend."

"And how do you know him?"

"We've been friends since we were kids."

"Okay so you grew up together, does he live here in the neighborhood?"

"No."

Edna walked in with a tray holding four cups of coffee, a glass sugar dispenser, a small ceramic cow milk pitcher, and a plate with several cookies and slices of Danish and cake which she sat on the coffee table as she interjected herself into the conversation.

"Stanley and Joel have been friends for years, they're all a part of the same circle of friends, been together since grade school, haven't you, Joel."

"Mom, please, this is my interview, let me tell the detectives what they want to know." Joel said to Edna in a rather childish tone and manner.

"Okay, okay, I'm just saying… These kids have been friends for years, the whole circle of them, all good kids, and all good friends."

"Mom, please."

"Okay, I'll excuse myself back into the kitchen. You men talk, and let me know if you need more coffee, and I'll bring it right out."

"Yes, thank you, Edna." Tommy said.

"Yes ma'am." From Clay, who then again began to ask Joel more questions.

"So, you were going to tell me where Stanley lives Joel."

"He, he lives in Hell's Kitchen, by himself, in a rooming house on Eighth Avenue off 36th Street."

"What's his last name?"

"Rosiello"

"And why do you think he told you about this attack?"

"He tells me everything."

"Did he tell you why it happened, Joel?"

"He didn't, but I think I know why."

"You wanna tell us?"

"Revenge."

"Revenge? Revenge for what?"

"Revenge for Wimpy."

"Okay, listen Joel…" Clay took a breath, shifted his eyes to Tommy for a second and then back to Joel. "Let's stop the back and forth here, and how about you tell me what you know about your friend Stanely and what he told you about attacking this gentleman the other night. Just go ahead and tell me the whole story as you know it."

"Yes, sir, I'm sorry, sir." Joels demeanor again becoming more solemn.

"No need to be sorry, son," Tommy said, "We're here to hear your story, hear what you have to say and hopefully get to the bottom of this case… you called us, remember? We are here to listen, Joel, please just tell us everything you know."

"Okay well I met Stanley back in Wagner Junior High School, and we were like in the same group of friends, you know, Stanley was, kind of a leader, you know like the tougher one in the group, and we all hung out together, and mostly played video games, sometimes watched movies, sometimes we all go out for pizza and a movie, you know typical friend stuff." Joel paused there and Clay prodded him along.

"And how many of you are in this friend group?"

"Well, there's me, Stanley, Wimpy, his real name is Paul, Butchy, his real name is Henry, and Chico, Chico's real name is Perry, and of course Frannie, she can be a bit much though, but she's still our friend unless she's hanging out with her girlfriend, Annie, then we don't see her, no one really cares for Annie, and we never hang out with her."

"Tell me about Wimpy and about this revenge, please."

"Okay yeah, uhm, well so Wimpy," Joel became slightly agitated as he began, "Wimpy, as you might guess from his nickname, my friend Paul, well he isn't a very tough guy, and never was, and, well he was beaten up by that man, the one Stanley killed … but there was really nothing Wimpy could do about it, so like always Stanley stood up for him, because that's what he does, he looks out for his friends."

"Wait, you're telling me, an 80-year-old man beat up on your 26-year-old friend Paul, so Stanley killed him?"

"Yes sir, yes sir, Detective, that is the truth, and I promise you, sirs, if you investigate that man, the man who died, you will see he is a very bad man, an evil man, a dangerous evil man, with an axe to grind. I know Stanley was wrong, and I know he took justice into his own hands, but what he did was out of loyalty, and friendship and love, and if you investigate that old man, you'll find out he was a dangerous and evil man." Joel said with a nod.

Clay sat back on the sofa in disbelief and Tommy leaned in.

"What can you tell me about Harry Greenblatt, Joel?" Tommy asked.

"Harry Greenblatt?"

"Did you not speak to Detective Volpe, about another case over the summer where Stanley beat up another elderly man? One you believed Stanely killed?"

"Yes, I do remember that. He was another dangerous man, a similar situation, almost exactly similar, almost exactly the same. Yes, of course, of course I remember that case, why, why wouldn't I remember that case?"

"Do you call 777-TIPS often Joel?" Tommy asked directly.

"Only when I know something awful has happened."

"And how many times have you called the TIPS number?"

"Oh, I don't know, maybe eight or ten times?"

"And these calls have all been in relation to what, Joel?"

"Murders, of course. I wouldn't call for something small, if it were something small, I'd call the precinct, unless of course it were an emergency, then you have to call 911, always call 911 in case of emergency, the precinct for smaller crimes, and 777- TIPS for murders, that I'm sure you know is the protocol."

Tommy pursed his lips, looked at Clay, then back at Joel.

"Joel, my friend, thanks for the information, and the insight into this case. I do appreciate your time, and the effort, as well as the coffee and cookies, I'm sure it wasn't easy coming forward and telling us about your lifelong friend."

"No, sir, it wasn't easy at all, but I know Stanley was wrong to do what he did, and, and I just wanted to do the right thing."

"I know you did. Detective Johnson and I are going to follow up on this and see if we can find your friend Stanley, as well as look into the backgrounds of these two elderly men, we have to head out on other business now, but thanks again for everything."

Joel again became almost joyful after hearing Tommy's words, he stood up straight and shook Tommy's hand, "Thank you, Detective Keane, I am so so happy I could help you with this case, and thank you, Detective Johnson, please call me if you need any more information. Remember, it's Stanley Rosiello, and he lives in a rooming house on 8th Avenue off 36th Street, he is pretty big and very tough so please be careful detectives."

"We will Joel," Clay replied, trying hard to be as pleasant as Tommy had just been and not call Joel out on the inconsistencies in his story, or on the fact that he was a chronic caller, and an obvious EDP (emotionally disturbed person.)

Tommy and Clay said goodbye to Joel and to Edna, as they left the apartment, and then stepped out of the building onto the stoop, where both men scanned the block from left to right before making their way to their car.

"That was a waste of a good hour, and look at you, making nice with the coffee and cookies… You've certainly softened over the years there, Two Gun."

"Hey, you know the old saying about more flies with honey than vinegar, and you never know, we may have to revisit these two nut jobs before this case is over. Not to mention, both are pretty sad and pitiful individuals, so no need to give either of them a verbal beatdown for jerking us around. It's obvious they're both out of their heads, and barely getting by, so yeah no skin off our nose, and no big deal we wasted a bit of time with these two… and stop with the Two Gun shit, before I kick you in the shin big man, I'm not afraid of

resorting to my tools of ignorance on your big ass if I have to."
Tommy replied holding up his fists as if taking a boxer's stance
as they walked towards their car. -

Clay smiled; he was really enjoying working with his old
friend Tommy again after so many years.

"So, what next? Any ideas?

"Yeah, next stop I think is Italian Village for a slice or
maybe some pasta and we do the old renew, review and
readjust, there's going to be something we're missing or haven't
looked into, but we'll discuss that over a little dinner, cool?"

"My man, I forgot just how much I like the way you
think!"

Chapter Nine

8:16 PM

Italian Village Pizzeria, 1494 1ˢᵗ Avenue.

Tommy parked the car in the bus stop just in front of the pizzeria, as they got out of the vehicle Clay said,

"Hey, this place looks different. You brought me here years ago, but I don't know, it just looks and feels very different, this the same place?"

"No, this is the new location, used to be a block and a half up. They had a fire and then opened this place, this is actually just my second time in this location, food every bit as good as it was, but I don't know? I just miss the old place."

"Sure you do, you have a history here, right?"

"Yeah, been coming here my whole life… and hey that being said, I haven't told anyone in the squad that I grew up around here, I only have a few months to go, and don't want there to be any conflict of interest bullshit, from the Captain or any other higher ups, you know how uptight this job has gotten, it's no huge secret, I just like keeping my personal life and business away from the job you know?"

"Do I know? This job has lost its ever-loving mind with every new rule and protocol, shit, motherfuckers be treating us like they baby sittin children while we out here fighting the good fight to try and keep these streets safe, please, you ain't gotta tell me about uptight."

Tommy laughed at Clay as they entered the restaurant and took a table in the back, he too was very happy to be reunited with his old friend and appreciated the unspoken bond men like them shared after going through life-and-death situations like the story Clay had told the other members of the squad on the morning of Tommy's return.

Over the last six months Tommy had become very fond of every member of his new team at the 2-1, even Sergeant Browne, and his personality flaws, but having Clay step back into his life after so many years was special, and somehow made the 2-1 now feel more like his precinct.

A round middle-aged Italian woman with glasses and an absolutely expressionless face took their order, Tommy asking for rigatoni Bolognese, and Clay the chicken cutlet parmesan, with a side of sausage.

"So, what you think, I mean about this whole case, not just our next step?"

Tommy paused for a second, then looking into Clay's eyes asked him the same question, "Let me ask you, go over it for a second then tell me what you think."

"I don't know man, I don't think we have a solid lead or suspect, which is a little surprising to me to tell you the truth. I expected we'd be onto something by now, the more I think about this, the more I want to look at the son David, maybe bring him in and stick him in the box (interview room) for a nice long talk, but I think after I have a similar long talk with the daughter Amanda again, just to see what more we can find out about them."

"I'd do the same."

"Could this also be some random antisemitic attack? I mean Volpe did just have a similar case right, old Jewish man hit in the head and knocked to the ground for no reason. I'm thinking we got to look in that direction too, get with Volpe, see what he knows then visit the other victim, what was his name again?"

"Greenblatt."

"That's right, Greenblatt, there wasn't much in that folder to go on, maybe Mr. Greenblatt can shed a little light on this case if it does indeed mirror his own attack."

"Yes, sir, I would do the same, anything else with what we got so far?"

"You know I'm gonna run the name Stanley Rosiello, fuck me if I don't, and then have him be the one running around town attacking old Jews, and we never looked into it, media would have a field day with that one, and headquarters would filet me, then station my ass out on Staten Island for the embarrassment I caused after being told he was the man."

"Haha, you know they would, and yeah man, you're spot on, I think that's our plan of action unless something else comes up? We'll head back to the house and set up interviews with Amanda, and David Abramowitz, as well as Mr. Greenblatt, get with Volpe, see if he has anything else that may not be mentioned in the case folder, and run Stanley Rosiello, and see what comes up."

***

9:22 PM

2-1 Precinct Squad Room.

Tommy and Clay entered the squad room and as they did, they found Sergeant Browne at Doreen Doyle's desk discussing a case, Jimmy Coletti typing away on another, and Mark Stein with his face covered by a copy of one of the day's newspapers.

"Hey, how'd you two make out today with that Abramowitz homicide? Any luck?" Sergeant Browne asked.

"We did some running around and got some interviews in, but I'm sorry to say I don't think we're any closer to finding our perpetrator just yet there, Sarge." Clay answered.

"No new leads? Nothing?"

"No, I'm going to look a little harder at the brother David, going to run him again and another name in the computer, set up interviews with him and his sister Amanda for tomorrow, see if we can flip a stone with either of them and maybe learn something we don't yet know."

"You need any help? Maybe with the computer stuff? I know your partner there is pretty much a useless dinosaur with the computer." Doreen asked, motioning her head towards Tommy who was leaning against Detective Keogh's empty desk.

"Why you gotta drag me into this?" Tommy asked, "You can't just be nice and ask if we can use some help? You gotta find a way to hurt me, make me feel old and useless? I thought you said you missed me? Looks like all you missed was someone to beat up on there, Detective Doyle?"

"Oh, come on now Mr. Man, let's not get our feelings hurt and our panties in a bunch…" Doreen began to respond but was interrupted by Jimmy Coletti.

"I know I missed you, Tommy. But Doreen was unbearable while you were gone, for the first two weeks she was all worried that you were seriously injured and not gonna return. Last couple of weeks she was bitter and spiteful because you weren't calling in to give us a day-by-day on your recovery!"

"Don't exaggerate, Jimmy…" Doreen began in her defense before Sergeant Browne spoke up.

"Haha! C-mon now, Jimmy's got it just about right there Doreen, you have been a little high-strung over Tommy's absence the last few weeks, and we've all been suffering for it!"

Mark Stein, chuckled softly from behind his newspaper, "You too, Mark?" Doreen asked, raising her voice slightly in order to regain control of the conversation, "Okay, we're done with this now," She said as her face began to flush with embarrassment, "Can I help you, Clay? Is there anything I can do for you pertaining to this case?"

As the rest of the room laughed a little over Doreen's consternation, Clay answered politely, although with a large cheesy smile, "Yes, please… If you could run this fella's name, Stanley Rosiello, possibly resides in Hell's Kitchen, twenty-five-thirty years of age, really, we don't know much or anything about the man, but it's a name we picked up today, and we need to check it out."

"You got it, Clay."

Clay called Amanda Shellsburg and made an appointment with her to come by the detective squad at 9:15 AM the following morning, for what he called a "Brief interview, just to dot some i's and cross some t's."

He then called David Abramowitz and set up a similar appointment also at the squad room for Noon and gave the same reason. Clay went to work running both Amanda and David's names every which way he could.

During his searches, Clay was able to find out all sorts of things about both Abramowitz siblings, from as far back as their high school years, through to the present. When it came to computers, Clay was definitely more capable than Tommy was and leaned well towards the proficiency Doreen held.

He found nothing suspicious or nefarious in Amanda's past, but David was another story, although nothing criminal, it would appear David was a mess when it came to his finances. He had regularly gotten deep into debt over the years, then magically would pay himself out of it, with no visible income to do it with, this, while not criminal on its face, certainly led Clay to believe he needed to look a bit harder at David as a possible suspect, as every detective is well aware, money is always top motivator when it comes to crime, and David Abramowitz, was once again deep in debt.

Doreen came up with numerous Stanley Rosiello's, however, she narrowed it down to three possibles; one aged twenty-one, who lived not in Hell's Kitchen but right there within the boundaries of the precinct on East 93rd Street. Another who was aged forty-four, who lived on West 11th Street, and a third who was aged thirty-two, spelled Stanly without the E, and he worked in a pizzeria located on 8th

Avenue, in the heart of Hell's Kitchen, his current address was unknown.

"Could it be?" Clay asked both Doreen and Tommy, "He lives in some SRO (Single room occupancy, a rooming house) and therefore doesn't have an actual address?"

"Sounds like our nutty friend Joel just maybe might be telling us the truth?" Tommy replied.

Both Clay and Tommy were a little surprised to find some truth to Joel's story.

Tommy and Clay decided the day had run its course, and they would reconvene in the morning; do the two Abramowitz interviews, pay a visit to Hell's Kitchen, and see if they could find Stanly Rosiello, and also visit Mr. Greenblatt, the survivor of the similar attack handled by Detective Volpe, several months prior.

Chapter Ten

It was just after 11:00 PM when Tommy hit the corner and decided it was a bit too cold that evening to walk up to his mother's place on 88th, so he buttoned up his tan-colored wool overcoat and hailed a cab. Tommy didn't direct the driver to take him to 88th though, instead, he decided to head over to 85th and York and have a beer and a shot before heading to bed. It had no doubt been a long day, but Tommy wasn't feeling quite ready to end it, and it had been several weeks now since he took a seat in Bailey's Corner Pub.

As the cab pulled up to the corner, and Tommy paid and got out of the vehicle, a sense of apprehension had come over him. He was looking, even hoping, to see Molly if she was working. But also felt like a bit of a rat. It had now been a full five weeks since Molly had come to visit Tommy at the Hospital in White Plains after the shooting, and in all that time he had only contacted her three times, and each time via text.

Tommy knew he was wrong to have, as he would have put it, "Left her on the dangle." Wondering about, not only his health but their relationship. Molly was a good and decent person, and although Tommy knew he was too old for her, they did have a very good, honest, and adult relationship. Over the last few weeks, Tommy knew he wasn't the one honoring that relationship and now felt apprehensive about possibly seeing her again when he opened the door to the pub.

Tommy took a deep breath and then exhaled as he pulled the door to Bailey's Corner open and stepped in, and sure enough there she was, every bit as beautiful as she ever was, buzzing around the full bar like a busy little bee, in her tight jeans and short t-shirt, smiling and laughing with the customers she was serving.

Tommy watched her for approximately two minutes as the guilt grew inside of him, when she looked in his direction and their eyes met, her beautiful smile left her face and she took a few steps down the bar where she pulled on Jack Norris', the other bartender's shirt, and excused herself from behind the bar.

Jack gave Tommy a head nod while stroking one index finger along the other in a tsk tsk, shame on you motion, acknowledging to Tommy that he knew he was in trouble.

Unlike how Molly would occasionally run from behind the bar and leap into Tommy's arms in the past, this time she marched toward him like an angry villager from a monster movie ready to do battle, and Tommy, not for nothing, was a little scared.

Molly hit Tommy with both her open hands hard in the chest forcing him to take two steps back, and then again putting him right out the door and onto the sidewalk.

"What the fuck is your story, Tommy?" she said quite loudly, just short of shouting. "Three texts, three fucking texts! That's all you could get to me over the last month and a half, you fucking fuck! I know we're not officially boyfriend and girlfriend, but fuck you, fuck you Tommy, we are supposed to be good friends, intimate fucking friends you mother fucker, and I give a shit about you!"

"I'm Sor…"

"No! Fuck you, I'm talking, you listen, you bastard, you were fucking shot in the head, they shot you, in the fucking head, Tommy. I was, we were all worried sick for you, you stupid motherfucker, I was afraid for you Tommy…" Her anger began to subside, and tears began to roll, "You stupid selfish motherfucker, three fucking texts, that's all I get, and then, you show up here? At my fucking job, fuck you, Tommy, fuck you, get the fuck outta here! Go on … fuck off! Out of my life! And don't ever come back! … Go on!" she shouted again, raising her arm, and pointing north up the avenue.

Tommy slowly turned and began walking up the avenue as Molly had demanded, he crossed 85th Street, and as he passed the entrance to Arturo's restaurant on the opposite corner to Bailey's, he turned as he heard footsteps running up from behind him, preparing himself for a blow. Molly leapt into his arms, just like she had done many times in the past, wrapping her legs around his waist. She hugged him with all her might and continued to curse him as she kissed him repeatedly again and again, still spouting curses at him whenever she stopped to catch her breath.

"Tommy, you motherfucker, I was so scared, I was so afraid for you. I, I don't hate you, Tommy, you fucking prick, I don't hate you, I love you Tommy, oh my god I'm so happy they didn't kill you, I was so so afraid Tommy!"

Molly grabbed Tommy by the face and turned his head, then ran her fingers over the area where the scar lay, just under his hair that was torn open by the bullet, it was just visible with the light from Arturo's awning shining down on the both of them. Molly's legs loosened and her feet met the pavement, but her hug tightened around him as she put her head deep into his chest,

"Will you come home with me tonight?" she asked softly.

"Is that what you want?"

"More than anything."

They walked back to the bar, and Tommy waited by the entrance, as Molly walked back behind the bar, wiping tears from her eye's she asked Jack if it was alright if she left for the night, Jack looked over at Tommy and then back at Molly,

"Go on, get outta here, you'll be no good to me now the state you're in." Was his reply.

"Thanks, Jack, you're probably right, you, you can keep my tips from tonight."

"Bullshit, your end will be in an envelope under the drawer waiting for you tomorrow."

"Thanks, Jackie, you're the best."

***

Tommy and Molly walked back to her place, and they made love, but this time, unlike every other time, it wasn't the fun, hot, lighthearted sex that they usually enjoyed, this lovemaking had a gravity and seriousness to it that Molly had never felt before with any other man. There was a bond, something deep, possibly even spiritual happening this evening, the near death of her older part-time lover, had changed Molly.

Her soul had aged a bit through the experience. She felt, as she lay naked atop Tommy, his arms lightly wrapped around her body, the soft beating of his heart in the ear that lay upon his chest, just how fragile life could be, how this man could very possibly never been able to lie beneath her like this again.

And a tear ran down her face and onto his chest.

Chapter Eleven

Tommy's eyes snapped open, the dappled light coming through Molly's laced curtains from the streetlight outside, he reached for his phone, it was 5:12 AM.

Tommy rolled over. Molly lay on her side, facing away from him, still naked from a few hours before. He slid himself over a few inches to be closer to her, brushed her soft strawberry hair to the side, and kissed her gently on her neck as he wrapped his right arm around her and gently pulled himself closer to her. 'You deserve so much better than me.' He thought to himself, then slowly got up and began to dress.

"Why so early?" Molly asked, not even opening her eyes.

"I have to go to work, Molly."

"No, stay… I took off last night, you take off today, that sounds like a fair deal to me?" Her eyes still closed.

"I can't sweet girl, believe me I would love to, but there is an old man in the morgue, who is waiting for me to catch his killer, and I can't just not go in today."

Molly opened her eyes, "Oh my god, does it ever stop?"

Tommy smiled, not a happy smile, but an understanding smile, the same one he used to give his ex-wife

Cookie, and other girlfriends he had after his divorce, "No, no honey they never stop."

He leaned over the bed and kissed her on the head, then she tilted her head up slightly and put her index finger to her lips and he kissed her for a moment on the lips, just long enough for her to feel he was sorry for leaving her.

***

Tommy headed up to his mother's place on 88th Street, and found her on her recliner smoking a cigarette, with a cup of coffee in her hand watching New York One News, as little JoJo jumped up at Tommy's waist again and again until Tommy picked him up and gave him a hug and a pet.

"Hey, Ma, how you doing this morning?"

"Tommy, Tommy, can you believe we're more than halfway done with March, and they say we might get more snow this year, Tommy, can you believe that?

"I'm doing good, Ma, thanks for asking," Tommy replied sarcastically, "No, Ma, I can't believe they're talking about another snowstorm this late in the season, but it wouldn't be the first time." He said as he leaned over, kissed his mother Maria on top of the head, and placed JoJo on her lap.

Maria Keane, never taking her eyes off the television, continued as Tommy made his way to the bathroom and turned on the shower.

"Tommy, the Middle East again Tommy, they're having trouble in the Middle East, again, will they never learn…"

Tommy yessed her a few more times as he went into his room and undressed. It had become a ritual now; Maria would start rambling about any number of subjects, wanting less and less to have an actual conversation, but just to get thoughts off her chest, and ideas out of her head, and Tommy would entertain her with replies and small talk, rarely engaging in real conversation.

His mother's condition was slowly deteriorating. Tommy had come to terms with it, he knew there would come a time when she wouldn't be able to take care of herself any longer, but he also knew there was absolutely nothing he could do to stop the progression of this awful disease, and he took solace in the fact that for the foreseeable future she was still able to get around fine, cook and clean, as well as make her appointments and make it out to the store on her own. Her current 'crazy old lady' state didn't worry Tommy, it was his mother's future he worried about.

He showered and dressed, then came out to sit with his mother for a minute, "There's a package for you, Tommy, a very nice young man, a teenager, dropped that off for you, Tommy, over there on the counter, Tommy."

Tommy stepped over to the counter and took the large, fairly heavy package in his hands, he noticed there was no address written on it, not one for him, nor a return address.

"Who delivered this, Ma?"

"Some nice young man, Tommy, looked about thirteen or fourteen years old, rang the bell and gave me the package, Tommy, he said it was for you."

Tommy's mind raced for a second, 'what was this suspect package, with no address, and a strange teenage delivery boy?'

He walked the package back into his room, gently felt it all over, and turned it upside down. It was an unwrapped untaped box, so he sat it on his bed, shooed little JoJo out of the room and closed the door, then gently lifted the lid of the box. Inside he saw what at first appeared to be brown leather, and then yes, that's exactly what it was, a brand-new brown leather Schott car coat, with a note that read, "Hey T, sorry they were all out of black, keep your fucking head down, -T."

Tommy smiled, the mystery of the box was solved, it was obviously a gift from Tommy's lifelong friend Terry Calahan, who most likely had his runner and protégé young Shane, make the delivery of this fine new leather coat, to replace the one Tommy had lost in the shooting.

Tommy pulled it out of the box and put it on, it fit perfectly, then he stepped back out to the living room and sat with his mother and little JoJo for a few minutes before heading out for work.

***

On his way to the precinct, Tommy stopped at H&H Bagels on 2nd Avenue and grabbed a dozen mixed varieties, with some butter and cream cheese on the side. He was running a bit late, which was unusual for the man who usually beat everyone else in each morning, but once he got talking with his mom and petting little JoJo on his lap, the morning somehow got away from him, and he figured a dozen bagels would make a fine excuse.

Meanwhile at the 2-1 squad Clay and Doreen had already arrived and began their day, as each detective opened a case folder, and began typing, the morning banter began,

"Hey, Clay, that was an awesome story you told us the other day about that shootout you and Tommy had up in the 5-3 when you two were in anti-crime, tell me something more?" Doreen asked.

"More? What would you like to hear?" Clay answered as he wrote some notes on a yellow pad.

"I don't know? Another cool story? Or no, tell me something about Tommy I don't know?"

"Something you don't know? Hmmm, do you know he still carries a torch for his ex-wife?"

"I didn't, so he's been divorced for like ten years, right? And still not over her?

"Nope, madly in love with her, and yeah, years since they split, but he still loves her."

"Wow, that's kinda sad?"

"Did you know he'll salute the flag when he walks by it, but only when he's alone, I don't know if that's a military thing, but once I noticed him do it, I looked out for it, and whenever he passes a flag, he throws a little salute, but he won't if he's with anyone."

"That's strange, only if he's alone?"

"Yeah, like it's a personal agreement of some kind? Always been curious, but I never asked," Clay paused in thought, "His daughter means the world to him, but that's not surprising, I think most parents think that way."

"So, tell me about the wife now? Does he not have any girlfriends? I mean is it like that, he only wants his wife? Because I've seen, when we were in the hospital a few weeks ago, I saw a few women show up who, well…"

"Haha, no, my man Tommy does very well with the ladies, his problem isn't getting them, his problem is not letting go of that damn Cookie, and it ain't her fault, she's a pretty sweet kid, it's just, you know, the heart wanting what the heart wants I guess?"

"Wow, yeah we don't know each other all that long, and he hasn't told me much about his past life or anything about his personal or love life."

"Tommy Keane is one of the most closed mouth people I know, it's one of the things I love about the man… and usually, when he does say something, he means it."

"Yeah, I can see that."

And with that, Doreen raised her eyebrow to the door as Tommy entered the room.

"Mr. Man! Look at you in your nice new leather jacket! How are you this morning?" She asked.

"Doing alright Doreen, Clay, how yous two doing this morning?"

"Doing good man, that is a sharp jacket," Clay responded.

"Thanks, I do dress to impress, I got bagels, where is Junior & Senior at, (Jimmy & Mark) they head out already? I know I'm a little late, but I figured everyone would still be here?"

"No, Mark and Jimmy had court, I signed them in so they could go straight down this morning." Doreen answered, "And it's just me today, so if you need any help with that homicide ask away, I got very little going on case wise."

"Okay great, well you can observe our interviews if you like, and maybe go with us to visit Mr. Rosielli and Mr. Greenblatt a little later if nothing comes up?"

"Sounds like a plan, Mr. Man."

Chapter Twelve

9:16 AM

Charice entered the squad room with Amanda Shellsburg, "Detective Johnson, we have a Mrs. Shellsburg here for you."

"Thank you, Charice, come on in Mrs. Shellsburg, can I offer you a coffee, tea, a soda, or a water perhaps?"

"No, no thank you, Detective, I'd like to answer whatever questions you have and then get back to work as quickly as possible, please, I, I've never been in a police station before, I have to say it's interesting, a bit scary, but interesting."

"Well, you have nothing to be afraid of ma'am, we're just going to ask you a few more questions and then you'll be on your way. Please follow me, we can have a little privacy in our interview room."

As they passed Tommy casually looked up from the desk he was sitting at and smiled, "Good morning, nice to see you again."

"Good morning, Detective Keane, very nice to see you as well," Amanda replied pleasantly, but it was obvious she was unhappy and uncomfortable about the circumstances of this meeting.

Clay and Amanda entered the box, and Tommy and Doreen entered the observation room to observe the interview.

"Wow, just like on TV, only a little smaller." Amanda said as she sat in the chair Clay directed her to sit in, "One moment, I need to get my folder," Clay replied, then left her alone in the room for a moment as he grabbed his folder, then made sure Tommy and Doreen were ready.

"Okay, Amanda," Clay began as he re-entered the room, "As you know, we're still working on your father's case, I wanted to meet again, mostly because you've had a little time now to come to terms with your loss, and maybe, just maybe, you've thought of, or come up with some new information that may help us in our investigation?"

Amanda paused for a moment, she was understandably nervous and looked it, as she fidgeted a little in her seat.

"You know, Detective Johnson, I have thought of nothing else over the last couple of days, and I am at a loss as to why anyone in the world would ever want to intentionally hurt my father. Everyone who ever met him liked him, he had a long career, never any iffy business dealings, he went to temple weekly, and now in his later years, really had a very quiet and simple life."

"And so far, that is exactly how it appears to us as well, but understand we have to dig into people's lives when things like these happen, and ask, well ask uncomfortable questions."

"Of course, please go ahead."

For over forty minutes, Clay went over Dr. Abramowitz's pedigree, he asked about everyplace he ever worked over the years, asked about friends and relatives, investments and financial information, and with each question nothing odd or leading in any way came up, however whenever he brought up her brother David, there was always an ever so slight change in Amanda's demeanor, something no one would ever notice, except for three experienced detectives, trying to solve a murder case.

"How close are you and your brother David?"

Amanda paused, "I would say every bit as close as most siblings are. We love one another, speak regularly, get together on the holidays, is there, is there a deeper question you're asking, Detective?"

"It seemed, and I could be reading more into this, but you'll tell me? That you, for lack of a better word seemed to be trying hard to keep your brother in line during our initial visit, can I ask you to tell me about that please?"

Amanda, obviously a bit nervous now, took a breath and paused before she answered. "My brother, Detective Johnson, is, can be, quite the asshole." She paused again, and starring down at the table began, "He is a suspicious, manipulative little man, who has no regard for anyone but himself, he mistreats everyone in his life, he has a deep if not desperate victim complex and places blame for every one of his shortcomings onto anyone in his orbit other than himself… I try, I try so hard to get through to him, but…"

"Listen, Amanda," Clay said softly, in a gentle caring tone, "We know your brother has been deeply in debt, several times over the last few years, and each time he seems to find the money to right the ship, can you…"

"My father of course! He and Rachel just live this ridiculous bohemian life, as if living in this world is free, and every time the debt gets too deep, my father comes up with 10-

20-30 thousand dollars to save little David once again, that all ended though, it all ended about a year ago," Amanda paused, she felt, she knew she had said too much.

"Go ahead dear, please tell me, what happened, how did it end?"

"Oh my god, I can't believe, do you think David could have anything to do with this? What do you know, Detective?"

"I don't know anything, Amanda, please tell me what you know, what happened between David and your father? – Please continue with what you were going to say."

Amanda wiped her eyes and took a breath, "He, my father, said no more. David and Rachel were again over their heads with spending, and couldn't keep up with their credit cards or rent, they had again put themselves into a very bad spot financially and my father simply said no, not again, and suggested David file for bankruptcy," Amanda paused again, "David made up a story about going to a loan shark and being threatened, but my father didn't believe him, he, he knew it was all a lie to try and guilt him, and in the end, well to this date, no one has yet to come after my brother other than legitimate bill collectors… You, do you think? Do you think David attacked my father?"

"Let me ask you something, Amanda, do you think David could have attacked your father?"

"Oh my god, I, my god I hate to think that way at all, but, oh my god, how can I even say but? But yes, I will say there is an outside, an outside chance that he is capable of such a thing, oh my god, yes, it is possible." She began to cry.

"Listen, Amanda, I want you to know that at this time I have no evidence of any kind against your brother, okay, you need to know that, we're looking into every possibility, and we did find David's financial situation, and history to be what you might call a bit of a red flag, but as of right now there is no evidence pointing in his direction okay. I think it's only fair that you know that dear… Please relax, I can see you're very upset, and I understand that, but please relax."

"Thank you, Detective Johnson, I'll take that into consideration, and I'll let you know if any new information comes my way, I'll definitely let you know."

Clay soon ended the interview, stood up and escorted Amanda out of the building, being as pleasant as could to her along the way.

If Amanda was visibly nervous when she entered the building that morning, she looked emotionally shattered as she left it, the thought of David's possible connection to her father's death was a painful, but plausible scenario that she sadly considered a definite possibility.

***

Upon returning to the squad room Clay simply asked flatly, "So? What you two think?"

"I say if his own sister thinks he may have killed her father, well then he may have killed her father," Doreen answered.

"Certainly, muddies the water a bit, don't it?" Tommy added, "This David, has two motives now, one is greed, in that he needs money and is sure to inherit something, and the other is revenge, the fact that his entitled little ass thinks his father has cut him off in his time of need, it's an old story, been told a thousand times. I think we got two things to do, one is getting a subpoena for old man Abramowitz' phone, so we can see if there were any convicting messages between him and David, and when David shows up, we grill him good, who knows? We know he's a weak individual, we may get lucky and crack this case right here in the box if we can get him to incriminate himself?"

"Alright, we got a path! And in an hour our boy David will be here, I think I need me a bagel and a coffee before he arrives."

12:21 PM

Charice stepped into the squad room, "Detective Johnson, aren't you a popular boy today? You have another visitor this morning sir, there is a David A-something down at the desk waiting for you."

"Abramowitz… Thank you, Charice." Clay replied, then asked Tommy and Doreen, "You two want to hop right into the observation room while I go get David? He'll never even know you're in the office."

A few minutes passed and Tommy and Doreen watched as Clay sat David down in the same chair his sister sat in a little more than an hour before. Unlike his sister, David entered the room with a cup of coffee and a bagel and cream cheese on a paper plate.

"Alright, David, as I said on the phone, we're just following up on your father's death, I know you were pretty upset the other day, and probably in shock over the sudden loss of your father so I wanted to get with you again to see if maybe you thought of anything you would like to add, or had any thoughts at all about this attack?

"Thoughts?" David said in a fairly non-caring tone and attitude, "No, I really haven't thought much about it at all."

Clay paused, this wasn't the kind of answer he expected to hear, "You haven't thought about it? – Your father's murder? You have no thoughts about it?"

"Well thoughts? Sure, some crazy smashed his head in and killed him, and that's it, he's dead now… that's about it, am I right?"

Clay, being the true professional he was, stayed calm and cool, even though David's flippant remarks were begging to be met with something a little less than kindness and understanding.

"You don't seem sad or upset, David?"

"I'm not, I mean, sure I loved the man, but this is New York, and these things happen, you know?" David said with an intentionally arrogant flair as he took a sip of coffee.

"I know you've had some financial problems, David," Clay began, not wanting to start his interview here but already losing his patience with David and his attitude, "And from what I understand your father refused to bail you out again? Can you tell me about that?"

"I don't see how that's pertinent to your investigation, or really any of your business, Detective."

Seeing that little jab struck a nerve, Clay decided to double up on it, "Seems to me, your father was a good and loving man, took very good care of his wife and children. Hell, he's bailed you out of your recurring financial jams straight through your college years and well into adulthood, and it seems to me you find his death to be little more than an inconvenience to you?"

"My father's occasional generosity, or lack thereof, was always on his terms, Detective, yes, he did help us out on occasion when times were tough, but he always made me ask, sometimes beg for money when I needed it."

"Correct me, Sir, if I'm wrong, but from what I understand your father paid for you to go to a private prep school, and university, set you up with a trust fund that currently pays you just over $6,000 a month in dividends, and has wiped your debts clean, from what I can see, at least five times, and to the total of just over $300,000… now by anyone's standards, it sounds like your father went above and beyond his parental obligations. Also, from all accounts, he sounds like he was a kind man who was loved by everyone he met, yet again you don't seem sad or upset in the least."

Clay struck another nerve and David sat up a little straighter, and in a smug, almost defiant voice replied.

"Should I be? I mean, yeah, he was my dad and all, but everyone dies, and this was just his time, I mean, yeah, you guys will hopefully do your job and catch his murderer, and maybe incarcerate some poor minority into an overpopulated prison system, and then as they say, justice will be served, I mean that's what we all want right? Justice for the old guy?"

Clay leaned back in his chair. He stared into David's eyes intently and thought for a second, 'This rude little fucker doesn't know the race of the attacker, it's not him, but let me break this arrogant prick and see if anything else spills.'

Inside the observation room, Tommy whispered in Doreen's ear: "Uh-oh, here we go, can you smell the wood burning? That's Clay's brain taking it all in, let's see now… Yup, here it comes…" Clay began to wring his hands, and then softly cleared his throat, "Let's see where he goes with it, Doreen." Tommy said excitedly as he watched his old friend maneuver his way through this interview.

"Minority? Why would you bring up minorities, David? Do you know something we don't?

"Uh, no, I, I just assumed…"

"You assumed it must be some black dude, right? I mean I know it does make sense; I mean fifty-two percent of homicides are committed by black men, ain't they, David? Is that what led you to that assumption?"

David's original flippant attitude immediately tightened up, "Uh, no, no sir, Detective Johnson, I just, well … I think it's actually a societal crime that so many of your people are incarcerated nationwide, and I, yes, I do, I would like justice for my father of course I would, but again not at the cost of one of your…"

"One of my people, David? One of my people? Let me tell you something about my people, David," Clay leaned in as far as the table separating he and David would allow, "My father and mother have never been incarcerated, I have two brothers, and neither of them has ever been incarcerated, I have three boys of my own, and none of them have ever been incarcerated, nor has my wife, nor has any of my sixteen cousins, or to my knowledge, any of their extended family members either… So, Mr. David Abramowitz, of this here upper east side of Manhattan, let me ask you bluntly, after your eight years of college, and vast worldliness, what do you think it is you know about my people?"

"I, I, I, I'm sorry, I didn't mean to hurt, or insult, or, or, I am so sorry, Detective, I just…"

"Here is a question for you, Sir, something we do know, and this is not me casting any racial dispersions upon any race, it is simply a fact, one that we have several witness statements corroborating, are you ready for it, Mr. Abramowitz?"

David, now visibly shaken, and tears beginning to well up in his eyes, "I, I don't know, what?"

"The man who attacked and killed your father was a white male, and he was your height, your weight, with your color hair… in other words you fit the description, and to a T, Mr. Abramowitz."

David shrieked like a woman, "Noooo, you can't be serious, no, it wasn't me I swear, it wasn't me. I loved my father, no, you can't suspect me, no no no, oh my, my poor daddy, I loved him so, how could you, how can you think that I…"

"Did you kill your father, David?" Clay asked calmly.

"No, oh god no! I can't go to prison for this!" He screamed.

"Prison? Did you kill your father, David?"

"No, I said no!"

"Did you have your father killed, David?"

"No! No, I had nothing to do with this, I swear!"

Clay stood up and shouted, "Did you kill your father, David!"

Again, a high-pitched feminine scream erupted from David's mid-section, "Nooooo I couldn't have, I wouldn't have, I was nowhere near there at the time, that's a fact, you can ask my wife!"

"Your wife?" Clay leaned back calmly in his chair, "You're not married, David, what else have you lied to me about today?"

David broke down a bit more, "Oh god, no no I'm sorry, Detective, that was a lie. No, I'm not married, I'm not…" he took a deep breath in an attempt to regain his composure and wiped at the snot dripping from his nose, "Listen, Detective Johnson, I swear, I solemnly swear, I did not kill my father. I did not have my father killed, my girlfriend Rachel can vouch for my whereabouts, as well as the doorman on duty in my building at the time, oh god, oh my god do I need my lawyer before you take me in? should I, oh my god should I make arrangements? …"

"What are you talking about, David?" Clay asked in a calm and relaxed demeanor just as he had when he started the interview some twelve to fifteen minutes before.

"Are you not sending me to Rikers Island now?"

"Rikers? No, David, of course not, you're not under arrest for anything, you don't need a lawyer, and you're not even in custody. I just asked you in here to have a quick conversation and maybe clear a few things up, and at the moment I think we're pretty much done."

"Am I, am I free to go?"

"Free to go? Of course, you were free to leave the second you walked in today. Again, I just wanted to ask you a few questions to clear a few things up, so yeah, I'm satisfied now," Clay said in a cool and collected voice, but then put a rather stern face on and his voice became slightly deeper and more serious, "Go on, get the hell out of here."

David let out a massive sigh, wiped his eyes and face, and scurried out of the room and the building as quickly as he could.

Tommy and Doreen exited the observation room, both with large smiles on their faces and Tommy shaking his head after witnessing the very quick dismantling and breaking of the very arrogant and spoiled David Abramowitz.

"That was quick." Said Doreen, as she high-fived Clay.

"Quick and quite brutal, so you obviously don't think he is our man then, do you? I can't see you letting him out of here so quickly or crushing him like that if you did?"

"No, I checked his alibi with the doorman, and he was home at the time of the attack. I wasn't sure if he hired someone, but then he let me know he didn't know the race of the attacker, doesn't mean he couldn't have still hired someone, who hired someone else, unknown to David whose race he would have never known. Still, the fact he thought it was a minority, when we know it was a white male, makes me think he's not going to be our guy, but I'm still going to keep digging on this little prick."

"Do you still think there's a chance he's involved?" Doreen asked.

"Always a chance, but at the moment, unless some new damning evidence is revealed, I'm not liking him for this. I think he's just a spoiled brat, who's taken advantage of his parent's and sister's love and generosity for years."

"Okay, next stop Pizza Suprema. Hopefully, we find our Stanly Rosiello behind the counter today, and hopefully he is our guy!" Tommy said, raising his hand and crossing his fingers for good luck.

Chapter Thirteen

1:38 PM

NY Pizza Suprema, 413 8th Avenue

Tommy, Doreen, and Clay all stepped into the pizzeria, hoping to find Stanly Rosiello. The place was very busy, and four men were slinging slices from behind the red granite countertops; two Mexicans, a younger Italian guy who couldn't have been more than nineteen, and a very short, very fat, balding Italian man with a receding hairline and a large mustache, who looked to be just over forty years of age.

Tommy asked the fat 40-ish man over the counter, believing he looked to be the most in charge, "Hey, excuse me, pal, are you the boss?"

"No, he ain't here, but I'm in charge of the joint at the moment, why? Who wants to know? You three cops? You must be cops, look at yous, what did the three of yous just walk off the set of Law and Order SVU?."

"You're right, we are detectives, and we wanna ask you about a possible employee of yours, you got a minute?"

"We gotta do this now? Look at us man, we're rockin' in here it's still part of the lunch rush, can't it wait?"

Tommy leaned into the counter, and as softly as he could, told the man, "A homicide waits for no man, come on out here and talk to us now."

The man's eyes opened wide, and he whispered back, "Homicide." Then shouted towards his staff, "Carlos, I'll just be a minute." Then as he stepped from behind the counter, "C-mon, let's step outside, these walls got fuckin ears."

The four of them stood on the sidewalk, away from the entrance of the pizzeria, and Clay began, "Listen, I know you're busy and need to get back to work, but a name came up in our investigation, and the only thing that's attached to this name is this business…"

The man cut Clay off with a bit of a -get to the point- attitude, "Yeah, well, so ask me, what's the name?"

"We're looking for a Mr. Stanly Rosiello."

The man's face went white, and he began to fall backward, as he did, he reached out and grabbed onto the sleeve of Clay's overcoat to balance himself. Both Clay and Doreen, grabbed the man by both arms to keep him from falling.

"Woah, are you alright?" Doreen and Clay simultaneously asked, "You cool? You cool man?"

The man caught his balance, shook his head quickly in an almost violent manner to clear his head… "That's me! You lookin' for me for some fuckin murder?" he said in a desperate voice, still holding tightly to the detective's arms.

"You?... You ain't six feet tall!" Clay exclaimed looking down at the short fat man.

"No, no I'm five foot four and a half inches!" Stanly gasped back.

"And you ain't thin?"

"No, I weigh 247 as of this morning!" Stanly said still in a panicked state.

"And you ain't 32!"

"Yes, yes I am thirty-two, actually." Stanly stated, in a less excited, and somewhat disappointed voice, as he let go of the detective's arms and calmed down as all four of them realized this Stanly Rosiello, was definitely not the Stanley Rosiello that the detectives were hoping to meet on this particular afternoon.

"Okay Mr. Rosiello, we're sorry for the scare, your name was given to us, with a possible 8th Avenue residence, and well, it led us here to your job, again, we're sorry for the scare," Tommy said.

"No, I don't live here, I live in Jersey. I left this shithole city years ago."

"Let me just ask you now, Mr. Rosiello, do you know your whereabouts, three evenings ago at about 8:00 PM?"

"Psst... of course, I was fuckin here, where the fuck else would I be, I do like sixty hours a week in this fuckin place, you kidding me? I'm always fuckin here."

The detectives each shook Stanly Rosiello's hand, and then headed back to their car and Stanly back to his sixty-hour-a-week job making pizzas.

***

3:32 PM

331 East 71st Street

After Stanly Rosiello's interview, Tommy, Clay, and Doreen, headed back uptown to 398 East 71st Street, the residence of Mr. Harrold J Greenblatt after Clay called and confirmed he would indeed be home.

They parked their vehicle by a fire hydrant near the building and made their way up to Mr. Greenblatt's 3rd-floor apartment.

"Hello detectives, hello, please, please come this way," Is how they were greeted by a white-haired head wearing a yarmulke poking out from a doorway a few doors down the hall from the elevator.

"Hello, sir, I'm Detective Johnson, we've spoken on the phone, and these are my colleagues, Detective, Keane, and Detective Doyle, we're from the 21st precinct, and like I said we'd like to ask you about the attack you suffered over the summer if you don't mind?"

"No, of course, I don't mind. Please, Detectives, please come inside, can I make you some tea?"

"No, sir, we're fine, we just have a couple of questions for you then we'll let you get back to your day sir."

"Say, young man," Mr. Greenblatt turned his attention to Tommy, "Are you the Detective I read about who saved those children on Thanksgiving Day? And who brought down that gang of Chinese just a few weeks ago... Is that you?"

"Yes, sir, I am that Detective Keane."

"Well, let me shake your hand again young man, it is very nice to meet you, sir."

"Thank you, Mr. Greenblatt, but although my name was in the papers, I can't take all the credit sir, my partner Detective Doyle here, was with me throughout both of those cases, and without her, well sir, I would have been lost."

"Is that so, well let me shake your hand again too young lady, and let me thank you for keeping us safe, I know these are trying times… Now what can I do for you detectives?"

Clay asked Mr. Greenblatt several questions about what he could remember from his attack several months prior, and what if anything he could remember about his attacker, everything he said matched what was already in Volpe's case folder, and the description roughly matched what they had from the Abramowitz attack.

A white male, about six feet tall, leather jacket and foul language, everything was almost exactly what the witnesses said at the scene, and the detectives were sure it had to be the same assailant.

But what struck all three Detectives, as they all listened to Mr. Greenblatt give his statement, is just how much he resembled Mr. Abramowitz.

Both appeared to be the same height, same build, and same hair, both wore yarmulkes, and at that moment Mr. Greenblatt was wearing very similar clothing to what Mr. Abramowitz wore at the time of his attack.

Nothing was said about this until after everyone said their goodbyes and thanked Mr. Greenblatt for his time and cooperation, but the moment they entered the elevator and the doors closed, Doreen began,

"Hey either of you notice…" and she was cut off by Clay,

"This guy looks exactly like the other guy!"

"Yeah! That's exactly what I was going to say!" Doreen replied.

"They could be brothers," Tommy added.

"Weird," Doreen replied.

***

The three returned to the 2-1 squad room, and continued to discuss the case and where it was heading, or more accurately how it had stagnated.

Clay and Tommy, who both didn't have strong suspicions on either David or his sister Amanda, for their father's death, agreed that David did have a motive, and possibly more than one, them being, David's debt, greed, and inheritance, and less likely but very possibly revenge, for refusing to continue to bail David out.

They also both thought there may be an outside chance, albeit a very outside chance, his sister Amanda could also be involved, if not directly, but by knowing of a crime and covering it up, and that possibility could also be concerning their inheritance.

So, this was the angle they decided to revisit, by digging deeper into both siblings' finances, as well as the fathers. Doreen was in complete agreement that at that moment that was the only connection that made sense, and she began computer searches on both.

While the three clicked away at their keyboards, Detective Volpe from A Squad walked in with a handcuffed perp in tow, opened the cage and shoved the perp in then uncuffed the man and told him to take a seat, closing the cage door and locking the criminal in.

"Hey, how we doing, everybody?" Volpe asked. "Any headway on that homicide you guys were asking me about?"

"Nah, man, nothin but dead ends," Clay began, then gave Volpe a full rundown of the investigation to date, and the whole office laughed, even the perp in the cage, about Stanly Rosiello's interview outside of the pizzeria, then towards the end of the run down when Clay mentioned visiting Mr. Greenblatt, Doreen chimed in, "Yeah, it was weird, Greenblatt, and Abramowitz, looked exactly alike?"

The smile left Volpe's face and he cocked his head to one side the way a curious dog would.

Tommy then said, his eyes glued to his keyboard as he typed away, "They could have been brothers."

Volpe stood up a little straighter, and something caught his attention, "Hey, you guys went to that crazy fucker's apartment right?"

"Who's?" Clay asked.

"That young Friedleman kid, Joel, the nut hatch chronic caller with the crazy mother, did you interview him in his apartment?"

"Yeah, we did, Tommy and I both, why what's up? You know something?"

"Well, I remember being in their place, interviewing them both, and there was a photo, like an 8x10 on an end table and I remember, I remember thinking, might even have mentioned it, I don't know? But the kids' grandfather, the crazy mother's father, he, he looked just like Mr. Greenblatt, obviously, I couldn't compare heights, it was just a photo, but just like you said Tommy, they could have been brothers."

"That's pretty weird?" Doreen said.

"Could there be a connection?" asked Tommy.

"I don't know man, this is sounding a little fantastic, we all met him, all but you, Doreen," Clay began, "Kid seems completely harmless, a crazy, chronic caller sure, but I don't see how he would fit into the mix. Now that being said, he did call in both attacks, didn't he? He did, and that certainly connects him in some way, hell, we all interviewed him, man, we gotta go talk to this kid again!"

"Call him in, Clay," Tommy said, "Bring him into the house, and we'll interview him here in the box and have it all recorded this time."

"Yeah, yeah of course."

Clay put the call in, "Hello, Mrs. Friedleman, how are you dear, this is Detective Johnson from the 21st Precinct, may I speak to Joel, please… Great thank you… Hey, Joel how are you? Do you think you can make it over here to the precinct? I have some more follow-up questions regarding the Abramowitz case… Very good, I look forward to seeing you then."

"So, when's he coming?" Tommy asked.

"He's on his way, hopefully be here in twenty minutes or so."

Chapter Fourteen

5:18 PM

PAA Janice Quaid entered the squad room, Charice Tate, being done for the day. "Detective Johnson, there's an Edna and Joel Friedleman, waiting for you downstairs."

"Okay, thanks, Janice," Clay hopped to his feet, "Fucker brought his mom along."

"That may be good, Clay, she may be able to add to this, maybe we can interview her separately, see if there are consistencies or contradictions in his story," Tommy replied.

"Damn! You are right again, man, yeah, we can double-check him if we think he's lying to us."

Clay escorted Joel and Edna up the stairs and into the squad room, and by all accounts Joel seemed thrilled to be entering the realm of these detectives.

Joel began as soon as he walked in, with a huge smile on his face, "Hello, hello everyone! Detective Keane," he said reaching out to shake Tommy's hand, "And oh my! Detective Volpe, so nice to see you again, sir! Hello, miss, my name is Joel, and this is my mother, Edna," he said reaching out to shake Doreen's hand.

"Hi, Joel, I'm Detective Doyle, nice to meet you."

"Ahh, another detective, very nice, very very nice, it is very nice to meet you, Detective Doyle."

Doreen smiled broadly, Joel was so happy to be there in the squad room, and almost seemed proud to be there with his mother, he felt a sense of validation entering the room. The fact that this small group of detectives actually wanted him to visit, and hear what he had to say, made him beam as if he were a high school athlete who had just scored the winning point to win his school a championship.

Edna also smiled as she greeted everyone, her son's happiness and apparent validation were certainly a comforting testament to her son's vigilance in watching over their neighborhood and reporting on every perceived crime and violation that took place.

Clay sat Edna with Doreen and offered both Edna and Joel some coffee, tea, water, or soda, Edna accepted a coffee and Joel took a can of Pepsi, and then Clay and Tommy escorted Joel into the box, and had him sit in the far chair behind the table, Clay taking the seat across from him, and Tommy sitting on the bench against the wall that was opposite them both.

Clay began, "Like I said on the phone, Joel, we called you in today to kind of elaborate on our previous interview and see if you can clear anything up or add to what you've already told us."

"And I am ready!" Joel replied with the enthusiasm of a game show contestant.

"Okay then, here we go, I wanted to follow up a little, and just confirm, how did you know about the attacks you called in on Mr. Abramowitz, this week, and on Mr. Greenblatt over the summer?"

"Yes, Detective," Joel spoke in an almost formal manner, wanting to be as professional as possible, "As I told you at our prior meeting, at my residence, I had secondhand knowledge of these assaults, and homicides, that were conferred to me by an acquaintance name Stanley."

"Stanley Rosiello?"

"Yes, Detective, one Stanley Rosiello."

"And how do you know Stanley?"

"I have known him my whole life, sir."

"Your whole life? Wow, that's a long time, so you two are friends?"

"I would say we are acquaintances, sir, we do share friends in common."

"And you believe that Stanley Rosiello committed these crimes."

"I know it for a fact, Detective Johnson."

"How are you so certain?"

"Stanley told me he committed them, he told me he killed that man over the summer, and he told me he killed that man this week, and that's why I called these crimes in. I know some would say I'm a rat, but I don't think murder is acceptable in society, I don't think any crimes are acceptable in society. We live in a country of laws, and if, or when someone breaks these laws, they must be held accountable, especially murder sir, even if it is someone you consider to be a friend."

"We couldn't agree more, Joel, could we, Tommy?"

"Absolutely, I couldn't have said it better myself."

Joel smiled broadly.

"Now tell us," Clay continued, "Why would Stanley confide in you, especially to committing a murder if you were only as you say, acquaintances, and why did he say he committed these attacks, did he say? Do you know?"

"Yes, sir, Stanley, well Stanley considers himself, well I guess he is kind of the leader of our group. He's the biggest and the toughest, he has a longtime girlfriend and kinda likes to decide what we're going to do when we get together, and in a way is sort of our protector too. I'll give him that, he does look out for everyone in our friend group."

"Okay, but that's not really answering the question, Joel, why would he confide in you?"

"He trusts me, Detective, that's all I can say, actually we all trust each other, that's why we've been together so long. I mean you guys, especially the police know how important it is to have friends you trust, you know people you can really count on when you're in need, well our group is like that, we're all good that way, and so yeah, Stanley trusts me, he trusts us all and that's why I know because he told me so."

"Yeah, I get that now," Clay replied, "did Stanley tell you why he attacked these men?"

For the first time, in the interview, Joel paused, it was obvious he knew something but didn't want to let it out.

"Joel?" Tommy asked softly.

"Stanley was looking out for our friend Wimpy, again."

"Again? Ok, tell us about your friend Wimpy."

"Yes, Wimpy, is our friend Paul, and he's well what can I say, he's kind of a wimpy guy, that's why we call him Wimpy. We're not being mean, we all love him, and Stanley loves him and looks after him like a little brother, but Wimpy is the one, well he's always, I mean always, getting himself into trouble. He always is the one who says the wrong thing, or makes too much noise or, I don't know puts himself in a bad spot, and then ends up taking a beating, and the poor guy, he's just a short skinny nothing, and he gets so scared, because he always has to take a beating, and is just too small to protect himself, so yeah Stanley, Stanley always stands up for him whenever anybody picks on him.

"Let me see if I can put something together here," Tommy asked, "Do you think that Stanley attacked these men on Wimpy's behalf?"

"Oh yes, absolutely, I'm sorry if I wasn't clear, Detective."

Tommy looked at Clay, and Clay back at Tommy, there was something amiss with this story, they weren't sure what, but they continued.

"Okay Joel, can you tell us why Stanley attacked these men for Wimpy?" Clay asked.

"Because Wimpy told him too, okay, not so much that he told him too, but more like he pointed these men out to Stanley because they had abused him. Which, of course, made Stanley mad, and also made Fran mad, so she encouraged Stanley to go after these men, and well for Stanley... Let me tell you, Stanley, as tough as he is on the outside, really is a good guy on the inside, and he really does try so hard to do the right thing by all of us in the friend group, and with Fran encouraging him… With Fran encouraging him, well I'm here to tell you Stanley is capable of anything."

"Including murder?"

"Including murder, Detective Johnson, that's why we're all sitting here."

All three men paused for a second and took a breath, then Tommy asked Clay to step outside for a second.

"We'll be right back, Joel; can I get you another soda? A candy bar, we may even have some bagels left if you'd like one?"

"Sure, a candy bar would be very nice, thank you, Detective Keane, and any kind, I'm not picky," Joel said, still beaming with pride, over being invited in to give this interview.

***

Tommy led Clay over to Doreen's desk where she sat chatting with Edna, "Excuse me, ladies, I don't want to interrupt, but I want to ask you, Edna, what can you tell us about Joel's friends, about Stanley and the others?"

"They're a good bunch of kids, Joel is lucky, he's had the same friends since grade school, and they all treat Joel so well."

"So, you know them all for years then, Stanley, Fran, Wimpy?" Tommy asked.

"Oh, yes, and all the others, it's not often anymore, but oh I love it when Joel gets them to come out. I, I just love visiting with all of Joel's friends, they are all such a bunch of characters, and they all make me laugh."

"Do me a favor, if you could, Edna, tell Detective Doyle here about the whole friend group, and she'll make a nice list for us in case we need to contact any of them regarding this case."

"Okay… How is my Joel doing? He is so excited to be helping you out today, thank you, thank you so much in believing in him and letting him help you, you know he calls in all the time about crimes that happen all over the neighborhood, I know Sergeant Ruffalo and him speak regularly."

"Joel is doing great, Edna, he is a wealth of information, hopefully we won't be much longer."

Tommy grabbed a Snickers bar from the machine, then he and Clay made their way back to the box. Before entering, Tommy sent a text to Doreen, "Make a list of all the names she gives you then do us a favor and run them all, I now think there is a Stanley, and if we can't locate him, maybe we can get to him through one of the others?"

"Got it!" She replied.

Tommy then told Clay what he was thinking, "Sorry, Clay, I just had a thought and wanted to get Doreen working on it. Obviously, this kid is nutty and a chronic caller, but I'm beginning to think there may be some truth to his story, and maybe if Doreen can find one of these other friends and we can get one of them to corroborate Joel's story, and even better give us an actual address where we can find this fucker Stanley, we'll be in business."

"Sounds like a plan, anything you want to ask him next?"

"I think we make a list of all his friends, something we can compare to his mothers, and just keep the conversation going, the kid loves being here, let's just keep him happy and keep him talking."

Both Clay and Tommy re-entered the interview room and took their seats.

"Sorry, we needed to take a quick break, Joel, here's your candy bar, do you need to go to the men's room or anything?"

"No, I'm good, and thank you very much, I love Snickers."

"Let me ask you, Joel, if you know? Both men that Stanley attacked were of the Jewish faith, does Stanley dislike Jews?"

"No, of course not. If Stanley was an antisemite, he wouldn't hang out with me, would he, or our friend Butchy. Butchy and I are both Jews, and we're all good friends."

"So, you don't see any connection then, as far as anything to do with these two men both being of the Jewish faith?"

"No, sir, the only connection I see, or know of, is that Wimpy pointed them both out to Stanley, for abusing him."

"Hmm, can you give me… let me ask you, I'd like to make a list if I could, just so I can keep everyone straight, and maybe make some notes. Can you name each of your friends, everyone in the friend group you've been telling me about that is?"

"Of course, well there's me, Stanley obviously, his girl Fran, Wimpy…"

"And Wimpy's real name is?"

"Paul, and his last name is Murgalo, and Butchy's last name is Weinstein, his real first name is Henry, Chico's last name is Tyrell, and his real first name is Perry, and Fran's last name is Malincanico, and that's really it for our group, we never see Annie anymore, because we all decided we didn't care for her."

Tommy made a quick list of all these names and excused himself, leaving the interview room and handing the list to Doreen, "Everything cool with you ladies out here?"

"Yes, we're having a fine time, thank you." Edna said with a smile, seemingly every bit as happy to be spending this time with the detectives in the squad room as her son was.

"Yes, Tommy, Edna here is a delight," Doreen said, also with a large smile, obviously enjoying their visit, and Edna's quirky nature.

***

Prior to Tommy's interruption, when he delivered the list, Edna had been telling Doreen all about Joel and his friends.

"Oh my, do those characters make me laugh, and they always have. Some of them because they are outright funny, like that Butchy, oh my god it's like sitting with a comedian, always cracking jokes and being so, so sarcastic. I like sarcasm, when it's not mean, of course, and then the others, that Frannie, oh she is a sweet kid, but her, I laugh at her, and at Stanley with the things they say, oh my god they are all such characters, and my Joel, ahh, he is so lucky to have them in his life, oh they entertain us so.

***

Tommy let himself back into the interview room and the conversation continued.

"Okay, and let me get this part right," Clay began, "You just mentioned that these two men abused Wimpy, do you know how, how did these men abuse Wimpy exactly?"

"They beat him senseless, repeatedly, again and again. They beat him till he was bruised and bleeding… And for no good reason, just for fun, they were, sadistic, absolutely sadistic."

Clay leaned back in his chair a bit, trying to understand, "These two old men severely beat your friend? Your friend who is a grown man, so badly that Stanley had to go after them? I don't think I can be…"

Joel interrupted, "No, sir, you don't understand. This happened when Wimpy was a child, I'm sorry if I didn't make myself clear, this…this all happened, it all happened years ago when Wimpy was a kid, and these individuals, they would regularly beat Wimpy, for no reason but their own sadistic pleasure, they abused him terribly, so these attacks you see, they are revenge for past transgressions. Wimpy, after years, identified these men and that's why Stanley took action and did what he did."

Just as Joel was finishing up that bit of his story, Tommy received a text from Doreen, "You guys need to see this!"

Chapter Fifteen

Tommy and Clay stood behind Doreen staring over her shoulder at her computer screen in absolute disbelief.

"What the fuck is this," Tommy said in a low but very firm voice.

"This is some kinda bullshit, alright!" Clay replied.

Doreen sat with her arms folded, her eyes darting back and forth between the computer screen and Edna Friedleman's eyes. It was obvious Doreen was upset, and now both Tommy and Clay joined her in her disappointment and growing anger.

"Kids got some answering to do," said Tommy as he began to march back to the interview room, "Doreen, keep an eye on this one."

"You want to rip into this kid or shall I." Tommy asked Clay.

"I'll be the bad cop, Tommy, you keep an eye out for any responses we need to take note of. And if you need to, go ahead and be the good cop and sprinkle a little sugar on this little fucker in the event we need to sweeten him up a bit after the verbal beat down, I'm about to give him."

Tommy and Clay took the same seats they were in previously, both sat and took deep breaths, then Clay began, staring into Joel's eyes, with a face full of contempt he sternly said.

"What the fuck is wrong with you, Joel? What kind of sick fucking game are you playing?"

"W-What? What are you asking me, Detective Johnson?" Joel's face went pale, and his eyes widened in fear of Clay's aggressive question, and at the apparent loss of any sort of rapport he thought he had with these detectives, who now appeared to be very unhappy with him.

"Do Detective Keane and I look like fools to you, boy? Do you know it's a crime to place fake calls, make phony police reports, and waste the time of the police?" Then raising his voice considerably. "Do you, Joel? Because of your crazy bullshit, Detective Keane and I have wasted hours chasing bullshit leads, when we could have been chasing after an actual murderer! Detective Volpe wasted hours as well this summer, is this how you get your jollies, son?" Then lowering his voice to a low but very threatening tone, "If I weren't the seasoned professional I am, I just might beat you half to death right here in this room you little game-playing motherfucker!"

Joel slid his chair back the few inches it would go until it hit the wall, "No, Detective please, I, I don't know what you're talking about, why are you so mad, why are you doing this, why are you being so mean…"

Joel was very shaken, and visibly upset, but then like a light switch going on, he froze, then rolled his neck and straightened his posture and took a more confident stance, and with a tougher, street kid vernacular he again began to speak.

"Leave the kid alone."

"What?" Clay asked.

"Yo, you heard me, big man, leave, the kid, alone."

"Are you kidding me?" Clay glanced quickly towards Tommy and then back to Joel.

"No need to check with your girlfriend, tough guy, your problem is sitting right here. That's right, this is between me and you now. You like to pick on people smaller than you, huh? Well, how about now? You tough enough to stand up to me? Huh? I'll break your friggin' head right here, big man, I don't sweat you, I don't sweat you one bit.

"Why you little mother…" Clay began to rise, and Tommy reached out and put his hand on his forearm, and Clay sat back down, and with that Joel stood up out of his chair and backed into the corner with his fists clenched.

"That's right, sit back down, big man, listen to your partner. It's obvious to me, he's the smart one, and he's lookin' to keep you from taking a serious ass stompin' right now, so sit down, close your mouth and quit pickin' on the kid."

"How about you sit back down now, there's no need to get excited, we're just having a conversation remember?" Tommy said in a cool and calm voice.

Joel unclenched his fists and slowly took his seat, and again began to speak with that same lowered voice and street kid vernacular, "Excited, I'm not excited. You two guys are excited, look at you, look at the both of you, bringing this young kid in here and threatening him, big man, big man aren't you," Joel continued, staring right into Clay's eyes, without one hint of fear. "Yeah, that's what I thought, you ain't so tough after all, are you big man? You're just another bully who likes to pick on and beat on little boy's aren't you?"

Tommy again put his hand on Clay's forearm as he leaned in slightly, a cocked his head in disbelief.

"Joel? Is that you?" Tommy asked.

"Joel? No, Wimpy has left the building, you two are stuck with me now, and if either of yous are still up for it, I'll gladly punch your teeth down your throats."

"No no, nobody's looking for a fight tonight… Can I, can I ask you your name?"

"You can ask me anything you want, don't mean I gotta answer… But yeah, sure, my name is Stanley, now how about you, who the hell are you?"

"Keane, I'm Detective Keane."

"Ooooh, Detective, big shot detective hey, that supposed to impress me? And how about this big ape here? He a cop too?"

"Yes, sir, he is, this is my partner Detective Johnson, do you mind if we ask you a couple of questions, Stanley?"

"What you wanna ask me?"

"Well, I'll make it real simple for you, Stan, you see we're looking to keep your friend Joel out of trouble, and we think you know something that no one else knows, and it could really help your friend… See we have been told, Stanley, that you attacked two men, one a few nights ago, and the other over the summer, what do you think of that?"

Joel smiled a crooked smile back at Tommy, his persona at the time not changing a bit.

"Eh, I think you got that wrong, Detective… You see, I only attacked one man, one miserable hateful man, you think you're smart, but you made a mistake there, Detective."

"Okay you got me, Stan, but can you do me a favor, and tell me how and why I'm wrong?"

"Yeah, sure I can, where you got your facts entangled, and what makes you wrong, Detective, is that I attacked the same man twice, once in the summer, and then again this week, when I saw I didn't get the job done right last year, so you know what, I'll give you a pass cause you're really only half wrong."

"Can you tell me what you used for a weapon?"

"Can I? Of course I can, Detective, the question is, will I."

"Fair enough, will you please tell me what you attacked that man with?"

"I like the please, very nice, yeah uh, I hit him with some D batteries in a sock."

"How many times did you hit him?"

"Oh jeese, that I don't know, between three and six I'll say? … Did I get that one right?"

"Sounds about right? One more thing, a favor if I can ask, please, actually not a favor for me, but for Joel?"

"Of course, I'd do anything for my boy Wimpy, what you need, Detective Keane?"

"Can you write the story down that you just told me on this yellow pad and then sign it for me?"

"For you?"

"Well, you'd be doing it for Wimpy."

"Of course, anything for that kid."

"Great, you see, turns out you're a good guy after all, Stan, thank you so much for your help," Tommy let Joel finish scratching out Stanley's confession and then asked, "I got one final question for you, do you know the name of who it was you went after? Or was it just anyone Joel pointed to?"

Joel became slightly agitated and responded again in Stanley's voice with a great deal of hate in his eyes. "Of course I do… It was that creep, Abe Friedleman. That malicious, sadistic, fiend of a grandfather who tortured Wimpy mercilessly until he left, and when we saw he was back, well, I knew I had to do something, to keep it from happening again."

Chapter Sixteen

At approximately 7:35, the interview was concluded, and Joel was held in the box and Edna in the squad room until the assigned ADA from the district attorney's office made it up to the squad to listen to the unbelievable story that had just unfolded.

Both Joel and Edna were removed from the 2-1 precinct and taken to the Psych Ward, at Bellevue Hospital. It was subsequently found that both had been under psychiatric care for decades.

Joel Friedleman had been diagnosed as a teenager with Dissociative Identity Disorder, DID, previously known as Multiple Personality Disorder. His psychiatrist believed he had as few as six, and as many as nine, different personalities living within him, the strongest of which was Stanley Rosiello. Stanley was Wimpy's protector and would do anything to protect Wimpy, the nickname given to Joel by his grandfather Abe, who oddly was a psychiatrist himself. He, who would ritually beat his grandson almost daily for no other reason than the sadistic pleasure of it, and whenever the boy would cry out, his grandfather would taunt him by calling him a wimp and regularly referred to him as Wimpy.

Joel's mother Edna, herself was a lifelong victim of her father, and yes, she did know and allow Joel's beatings to occur when he was a child, but she was at this point herself insane, and definitely more of a victim than an enabler of her father.

When Doreen asked Tommy and Clay to come and see what she had found on the computer, it was a Wikipedia page for the 1974 film The Lords of Flatbush, a page she was forwarded to several times while searching for the names of Joel's friends.

Doreen opened it after the third time she was forwarded, and had stopped on the section labeled cast, which read:

- Perry King as Chico Tyrell
- Sylvester Stallone as Stanley Rosiello
- Henry Winkler as Butchy Weinstein
- Paul Mace as Wimpy Murgalo
- Susan Blakely as Jane Bradshaw
- Maria Smith as Frannie Malincanico
- Renee Paris as Annie Yuckamanelli

Tommy, Clay, and Doreen immediately lost their patience with both Joel and Edna, after believing the two of them were playing games with them, but the stress induced on the fairly weak-minded and mentally ill Joel, as his interview intensified, quickly allowed for the appearance of his protector, Stanley, who in true Stanley fashion, stood up for the kid.

The detectives were still not sure what to make of the situation but did indeed believe there was more to it than what was obvious to them at the time, and they immediately sought both legal (the district attorney's office) advice, and medical (the trip to Bellevue hospital) attention, in order to close the case on Sol Abramowitz.

A subsequent search warrant uncovered a black motorcycle jacket in Joel's closet, inside one of its pockets was a white sock stained with blood and four D-sized batteries inside of it.

Although an arrest was made and the 2-1 Detective Squad had closed a murder investigation, the detectives involved gleaned little solace in getting their man. This case, as with many, had more victims involved than perpetrators, and the most truly evil individual involved in this case had left the earth from a coronary fourteen years prior and was now out of reach of the squad, or justice.

Epilogue

The investigation by the District Attorney's office, following Joel being taken into custody by the Detectives of the 2-1 Squad, found Joel Friedleman to have a lifelong history of mental illness.

His Doctor, Sharon Jefferies, MP concluded that Joel Friedleman suffered from the rare diagnosis of DID, (Dissociative Identity Disorder.) also known as Multiple personality disorder, brought on by years of physical and psychological abuse by his late grandfather Abe Friedleman.

Joel created new personalities to mentally hide himself in, in order to defend himself from all of the abuse and trauma he suffered as a young child.

Somewhere in his youth he saw the 1974 film 'The Lords of Flatbush', a coming-of-age film about a group of young toughs from Brooklyn NY. Joel identified with the character Wimpy Murgalo, quite possibly because when Joel would cry out during his grandfather's abuse, he would be called a Wimp, for not taking his beatings as a man.

As time went on, Joel adopted many of the cast from the film, into the characters of his own little gang that resided within his head, the character Stanley, being the protector of the group.

Joel would openly talk about these characters to his one and only friend in the world, his mentally ill mother, Edna, who not only played along with Joel's fantasies, but enjoyed the occasional visits from Joel's "Friends," who were not much more than weak impersonations done by Joel for both his mental stability and his mother's entertainment.

Joel would often say he was going to get pizza with Stanley and Chico, or to a movie with Butchy, when in reality he would go alone, although for him, and as far as his mother was concerned, he had a strong and healthy relationship with all of these characters he had adopted inside his head.

Several months after his arrest, a bench trial was held and Joel plead guilty by reason of insanity to the murder of Sol Abramowitz, and the 1st degree assault on Harry Greenblatt.

The Judge took into consideration the long history of mental illness, and treatment, Joel and his mother had and the absence of any prior criminal history, and so sentenced Joel to eighteen months at the Creedmoor Psychiatric Center, in Queens Village New York, where if, after his term he was considered not to be a danger to himself, or the public, he would be released and allowed to return home.

And that is exactly what happened. Today Joel and Edna live in the same apartment together, and with more frequent Dr. visits. Joel's chronic calls of fictitious crimes have gone from as many as eight a year to as few as two.

Authors Note

Multiple Personality Disorder, now currently referred to as Dissociative Identity Disorder, or DID, also often known as Split Personality Disorder, is a complex psychological condition that can be caused by many things, but most often is related to severe trauma during early childhood, often extreme, repetitive physical, sexual, or emotional abuse, where in order to psychologically protect oneself a person may adopt more than one identity. This dissociative aspect produces a lack of connection to one's thoughts and reality and is believed to be a coping mechanism where one can literally shut off or dissociate oneself from an experience that is too painful or traumatic to assimilate to one's conscious self.

While DID is a very rare condition, it is nonetheless a very real condition, where victims are able to hide and therefore cope with severe past trauma by passing their experiences onto one or several other personalities they have created.

Read on for a sneak peek at the next book in the Tommy Keane series:

William Tell

Tommy remained squatting over the corpse and began to study his victim and her surroundings. Heather Mills was an exceptionally attractive woman, with large blue eyes, well-kept long blonde hair, nicely applied makeup, and nails. She was dressed in tight jeans and high boots, with an expensive-looking waist-length lambskin jacket that had a faux fur collar. She was still wearing gold earrings, gold chains, gold rings, and what appeared to be an unopened purse at her side, all made Tommy immediately remove robbery as a motive for this crime.

As he continued to take in the scene, Doreen made it up the stairs, and they both stood next to one another staring down at the body,

"Damn, she's a good-looking girl," Doreen said, "I bet we're going to find out she's a model or an actress, no one looks this good and doesn't get paid for it."

"I'm going to agree with you there," Tommy replied, "Poor fucking thing, who would do this to you?"

Tommy notified Sergeant Browne and Lieutenant Bricks with what they found at the scene, and a few minutes later, Detectives Mark Stein, Clay Johnson, and Jimmy Colletti, joined Tommy and Doreen and aided in the preliminary investigation.

Crime Scene arrived and started their work, photographing the entire interior of the building's hallways, stairways, and landings, and printing every surface from the front stoop all the way up to the roof's landing.

Medical Examiner Kristin Smyth arrived on scene and concluded that Miss Mills was indeed dead, cause of death most likely the arrow that was lodged in her throat and asked that Tommy call her the following day for a time to come in for the autopsy.

As soon as Crime Scene and ME Smyth were through, Tommy and Doreen gave Heather Mills's body a thorough search. They recovered the keys to her apartment from her jacket pocket, her identification, credit cards, gym membership, different pieces of makeup, a small cigarette box containing two joints, and a small baggie with three little blue pills with SKY imprinted into them.

Tommy then took Heather's keys and tried each one until he was able to open the door to her apartment. Then drawing his .9mm Smith and Wesson from its holster, he looked back at Doreen,

"Be cool, don't touch anything, this may end up being part of our crime scene and we don't want to disturb anything, and if we decide we do want to disturb anything, you know we're gonna have to wait for a warrant anyway to really dig into this place."

Doreen nodded in agreement as she drew her .9mm Glock, and Tommy opened the door to Heather Mills studio apartment,

"Police!" He shouted, "Anyone in here? Police 21st Precinct NYPD! Let us know you're here!"

About the Authors

Travis Myers and Natasha Myers Marsiguerra are a brother and sister team who both grew up in New York City.

Travis is a retired New York City Police Detective, and Natasha works and lives in California.

Together they form a perfect team in that Travis, who has more stories to tell than a pub full of Irishmen, suffers from dyslexia and abhors anything to do with reading or writing. Natasha, his beloved little sister, is an avid reader of absolutely anything that is put in front of her and has been blessed with the gift of gab. She can out-story just about anyone, in any room, at any given time, and she can also type 60 words per minute. More importantly, Natasha is able to understand where her older brother is coming from, and craft his stories into a readable format.

Together, they weave the Tommy Keane Detective series into well-braided fictional tales that are nearly all based in actual events that they, and their friends and relatives, have lived. Travis and Natasha deliver on their promise to tell gritty, honest stories that are rooted in the everyday lives of everyday people.